THE SAINT IN PURSUIT

So it was that less than two days and half a world away from that brief conversation he sat relaxed – blackhaired, lean, immaculately tailored, piratically handsome – in the Lisbon Embassy, confronting a much less relaxed military attaché who was obviously inclined to fidget about incursions of civilians into his territory.

"I can't say this is a sentimental journey, exactly," Simon Templar said, "even if I do get a lump in my throat when I think of the American taxpayers footing my expenses. But it does take me back."

His quizzical blue eyes glanced over the panelled room, which was protected from the glaring heat beyond its wide windows by the best imported Yankee air-conditioning, and across the spacious mahogany desk at the officer's neat uniform. The officer fidgeted. He was a middle-aged man with reddish hair and a baritone voice whose low pitch seemed self-consciously cultivated.

"Were you here in Lisbon with the OSS during the war?" he asked with forced cordiality. "I – er – I haven't been filled in completely on your background."

"Nobody has," the Saint said simply.

Also by the same author,
and available from Coronet:

The Saint in Pursuit

Leslie Charteris

CORONET BOOKS
Hodder and Stoughton

First published in Great Britain in 1970 by Hodder and Stoughton Ltd.

Coronet edition 1989

Printed and bound in Great Britain for Hodder and Stoughton paperbacks, a division of Hodder and Stoughton Ltd., Mill Road, Dunton Green, Sevenoaks, Kent TN13 2YA (Editorial Office: 47 Bedford Square, London WC1B 3DP) by Cox & Wyman Ltd., Reading.

ISBN 0 340 51832 4

EXPLANATORY NOTE

Readers who have an uneasy feeling that they have "read" this new book before can relax again. They haven't. But they may be recalling the plot of the original comic strip on which it is based, which was syndicated by the New York *Herald Tribune* between July 17, 1959, and January 7, 1960. Of course, I wrote that, too.

L C

CONTENTS

I: How Simon Templar answered a
Summons, and Vicky Kinian
was Observed.

It is a philosophical observation so profound as to be plati-
tudinous, that a man's past is never finally past until he is
buried; that any encounter, any incident in his life, though
he may long since have filed it away as ancient history and
for all everyday purposes forgotten it, may only be waiting
with the infinite patience of a time-bomb to make violent
re-entry into the peacefully lulled passage of his days.

This fact has been discovered with grave discomfiture by
such diverse divisions of mankind as professional puritans,
retired embezzlers, complacent bigamists, signers of peti-
tions, devisers of unsolvable murders, and ambitious politicians who go into public life without first making sure
that certain smouldering letters have been permanently
extinguished.

In this episode of the chronicles of Simon Templar with
which we are about to be concerned, the bomb had been
planted during a war which ended a quarter of a century
before the fuse ran out of its length. And if he could accept

such a delayed resurrection with his equanimity ruffled by
little more than a raised eyebrow, it was because he was
within certain limits a resigned fatalist. If he had ever in
his adventurous life been subject to wild waves of hope or
unnerving attacks of apprehensiveness, he would never
have survived to enjoy the fame and more importantly the
fabulous fortune that his sallies as a twentieth-century Robin
Hood had earned him. But ever since he had made it his
vocation to prey on the world's bullies, crooks, and pompous
bloatpurses, he had accepted it as an inexplicable but in-
controvertible destiny that trouble would always come to
him even when he wasn't looking for trouble, and that the
only intelligent response was, in the words of the classic
parable, to relax and enjoy it. Considering the antipathy he
had aroused among both the Ungodly and their tax-
supported official foes, most people in his place would have
figured themselves stupendously successful to have stayed
alive at all. Simon Templar, called the Saint, had not only
survived but prospered in the greatest good humour with a
Zarathustrian confidence in his ordained eventual victory
over everything that the Ungodly could throw at him.

The first spark out of the past this time was a telephone
call that traced him somehow to a hotel in Tokyo, and a dry
voice that he had only ever known by the code name of
Hamilton and an unlisted number in Washington.

"I've got a little job for you," it said, "that should give you
much more of a lift than those geishas."

"I packed up my cloak and dagger in mothballs years
ago," said the Saint. "And I thought you'd have retired before you got senile."

"This is unfinished business," Hamilton said. "I'm having
a plane ticket to Lisbon delivered to you. If you can bear
to get out of your kimono, ask for Colonel Wade at our embassy there. He'll brief you."

"Just be sure it's a first-class ticket," said the Saint. "My days of patriotic economizing are over."

It would never have seriously occurred to him to refuse, and he knew that Hamilton knew it—just as he knew that Hamilton would never have called him out of that distant past without some irresistible reason. And that was all he needed to tell him that life had made a new move in the very special game it played with him, and there was a challenge that any true buccaneer must accept.

So it was that less than two days and half a world away from that brief conversation he sat relaxed—blackhaired, lean, immaculately tailored, piratically handsome—in the Lisbon Embassy, confronting a much less relaxed military attaché who was obviously inclined to fidget about incursions of civilians into his territory.

"I can't say this is a sentimental journey, exactly," Simon Templar said, "even if I do get a lump in my throat when I think of the American taxpayers footing my expenses. But it does take me back."

His quizzical blue eyes glanced over the panelled room, which was protected from the glaring heat beyond its wide windows by the best imported Yankee air-conditioning, and across the spacious mahogany desk at the officer's neat uniform. The officer fidgeted. He was a middle-aged man with reddish hair and a baritone voice whose low pitch seemed self-consciously cultivated.

"Were you here in Lisbon with the OSS during the war?" he asked with forced cordiality. "I—er—I haven't been filled in completely on your background."

"Nobody has," the Saint said simply. "We were all very busy in those days, weren't we, Colonel?"

He realized as he said it, with a certain shock, how inexorably it dated him. Time slips by with such astounding smoothness that we are seldom aware of the space it has covered until we count back. But a few of the Saint's ac-

tivities during that war have been inescapably recorded
in other volumes of this saga, so that some milestones cannot be hidden from any student with a mastery of elemen-
tary arithmetic.

"Yes, we were," was all Colonel Wade could think of to
reply. He produced a salesman's sudden depressing smile.
"Well, wherever you were exactly in the forties, Washington seems to think you're the man for this job now, and my
orders aren't to question you at all, of course . . ."

Most of the officer's sentences never seemed to come to
a full period, leaving the impression that he was about to
say "but—" He cleared his throat and unnecessarily straightened some papers on the desk in front of him. Simon
Templar waited, secure and cool in his own un-uniformed
independence.

"This—er—matter involves one of our Intelligence Officers,
a Major Robert Kinian, who disappeared here in Lisbon in
1944. He'd been to school in Germany for years, spoke the
language perfectly, and he'd been undercover there during
the first part of the war. Then in February of '44 he came
here and . . ." Wade flicked one of his hands. ". . . disappeared . . ."

"A lot of people disappeared in 1944," the Saint said impassively. "But I'd have thought that by this time you'd have
closed the file on an agent who disappeared on a risky mission in wartime."

The colonel pressed his hands together in front of him,
steeple-like, carefully matching the tip of each finger precisely with its opposite.

"If it was an assignment like Kinian's—never," he said.
"There was too much involved, and there are questions we
want answered because the answers could still mean a lot
today. We don't give up easily. If you see what I mean."

The officer showed quiet pride in American intelligence's

bulldoggery. Simon let him enjoy himself for a moment before deflating him as gently as possible.

"And just what have you found out about him in these last twenty-five years?"

The Saint refrained from bearing down on the number for the sake of good civilian-military relations. Colonel Wade nevertheless betrayed embarrassment. His homemade steeple crumpled and he smoothed his already smooth papers with nervous hands.

"We—er—we haven't found out anything, yet," he admitted.

"No clues at all?" Simon asked.

"No," said the colonel. "I can give you the whole story very quickly." He pushed back his chair, stood up, and paced the room like a university lecturer as he talked. "We know this: Major Kinian had been underground in Germany for six months in the second half of 1943. As I said, he knew the country thoroughly and spoke German like a native. He got out to Switzerland in February '44, but he didn't make any report there. He came on to Portugal a few days later— about the middle of February—and made a telephone call to report his arrival in Lisbon and the hotel he was staying at."

"Where was the call made from?" the Saint asked.

"From his hotel, presumably. The Avenida Palace. Of course we checked every possibility of tracing him through the hotel personnel years ago. His stay there was perfectly normal, it seems. Until after a couple of days he just didn't come back, and he's never been seen again."

"And that one telephone call was his only contact with the OSS?"

Wade nodded.

"It was his only contact with anybody on his own team. Since he was on an underground mission he never came here or met the fellow who had my job at the time. After

he telephoned, Washington waited two days for the report
he was supposed to send to the embassy here. Then an agent
was sent to contact him." The colonel made an empty-
handed gesture. "No dice. Nobody knows what happened
to him."

His story finished, the officer dropped back into his red-
leather swivel chair and stretched his legs.

"With so much to go on I should have the riddle unrav-
elled in half a day," Simon said caustically. "You left out
just one minor detail. What was this mission Major Kinian
had been on?"

"He was trying to get a line on the escape plans of the
Nazi bigwigs if they lost the war," the colonel answered.
"With Roosevelt pushing for unconditional surrender, there
obviously wasn't going to be much future for secondhand
SS officers, or Nazi politicians, in Germany. It was common
knowledge that the top boys were getting escape hatches
ready for themselves and salting away plenty of funds to
keep them comfortable in their retirement."

The Saint tilted back his own chair and folded his arms.

"I'm afraid, Colonel, that if Kinian was working inside
Germany on something as big as that, your predecessors
should've *expected* him to disappear. Apparently he was on
such a hot trail that he didn't dare take his nose off it—even
after he got into neutral territory."

"Right. That's the way we figure it."

"But the game got *his* scent about the time he got here—
and turned around and removed him."

"I'm afraid that's the most obvious possibility, Templar,"
said the officer soberly.

Simon stood up to his full six-foot-two and walked over
to the window. Somehow the spacious peace of the embassy's grounds, the summer sunlight in the foliage of the
trees, made the cruel deaths of the Second World War seem
almost as remote as the battles of the *Iliad*.

"And that was the end of the trail," he said quietly.

"The end of one trail," Wade replied, and went on with fresh enthusiasm: "We kept an eye on other possibilities—and his daughter was one of them."

"She must have been all of ten years old at the time," the Saint said, turning to face the man in the uniform. "An obvious Mata Hari."

The colonel allowed himself a disciplined smile.

"She was only one year old at the time, as a matter of fact," he said. "But being as she's the only member of Major Kinian's immediate family who's still alive—his wife died five years ago—we thought there might be a chance she'd give us a lead someday. And I think she has."

The Saint's interest had clearly picked up. He was following the colonel's words intently.

"Without wanting to impugn the honour of the secret services," he said, "I assume you're thinking that Major Kinian may have taken the back door to the rich life by joining up with the lads he was supposed to be undoing."

"It's a possibility," Wade said in his radio-announcer's baritone. "Very remote, perhaps. But we had to consider that and a lot of other chances to be sure we were covering the field. And now, just recently, on her twenty-fifth birthday, Kinian's daughter was given a sealed envelope by an attorney that's bringing her straight to Lisbon."

"From America?"

"Right. From Iowa. It wasn't her father's regular attorney who gave her the letter, or we probably would've known about it before. We checked him long ago. But we know the letter is from the girl's father, and that it was given to her on her birthday by a lawyer we didn't know he'd had any dealings with. A few days later, she quit her job and booked a passage to Lisbon—where *he* vanished."

"It looks a little as if Major Kinian was trying to out-secrecy everybody, doesn't it?" Simon commented. "You've no idea what was in that time capsule he left for his daughter?"

"I'm afraid not. Neither did the lawyer who delivered it. And we couldn't have gotten a look at it afterwards without a search warrant or a burglary—even if she hadn't destroyed it by then. But anything we did might have warned her that she was under surveillance, whereas the way things are it's probably the last thing she'd think of. We don't want to upset the apple cart at this point. Washington thinks you're the man to follow through on this, rope the girl and give her plenty of slack without losing her until you've found out what it is she's up to."

"I do have a deft hand with apple carts," Simon conceded, "and I'll even admit to a certain natural aptitude for keeping my eye on girls. Where's she staying?"

"The Tagus Hotel," Colonel Wade said. "Here's her picture. She only got in this morning, so she can't have done very much yet. And by the way, we've got you a room reserved at the Tagus directly across the corridor from hers."

"As travel agents you couldn't be more efficient," Simon murmured, as he picked up the snapshot from the desk. "And from the looks of this, even the entertainment on this tour is going to be first rate."

The colonel smiled, this time more genuinely than he had before.

"Well, enjoy yourself. Hamilton says that's one thing you can always be counted on to do. Call me if you need anything, but no routine reports are expected. And if you get in trouble, I never heard of you. You know the drill. The rest is up to you." He shook the Saint's hand briskly. "I hope we're not moving too fast for you."

"Not at all, Colonel," Simon said from the doorway. "There's nothing quite so likely to get me moving fast myself as a familiar aroma that's emanating from somewhere around here—the sweet fragrance of vintage loot!"

2

Vicky Kinian had the kind of sweet dark-haired beauty that brings to mind orchards in the sunlight of a dewy morning, and arouses in the bosoms of mature men an almost painfully adolescent nostalgia for girls-next-door such as never really lived next door. She had the lovely youthful aura that the modern alchemists of Hollywood indebt themselves trying to transmute out of gold—and yet the closest she had ever been to Hollywood was the projection on a television set. She was, in actual fact, the perfect coral-lipped rose that poets imagine blushing unseen in the desert air of Arkansas or the more inhospitable portions of Sardinia, and when she turned twenty-five the longest trip she had ever taken had been from Des Moines, Iowa, to Yosemite.

So that for her there was none of the world-weary sense of a routine errand that a great many of her contemporaries would have experienced on the June morning when she walked into a Des Moines travel agent's office to pick up an air ticket which was to waft her into considerably more hazardous excitement than International Airways customarily supplies along with its *tournedos* and Waldorf salads. And Vicky herself had known that she had more to be excited about even than a first trip to fabulous foreign shores. In her new handbag, along with her passport and vaccination certificate, was a third and more personal document—one she would show to no guardian of national borders and about which she had spoken to nobody—which promised mysterious developments in her life without giving any clue as to what those developments would prove to be.

And as she stepped into the travel agency that morning, a new disquieting ingredient had been added to the mix-

ture of anticipation and curiosity which had kept her awake
for several nights already. She stopped just inside the
agency's glass door, looked around at the dozen or so preoccupied people who were distributed on either side of the
service counter, and turned to her companion, a short and
shapeless, mousey-haired girl of the type that is foredoomed
by an unlucky shuffle of chromosomes to play a brief walk-
on bit in such affairs as this, and thereafter to be painlessly
forgotten by everyone except herself. To give her at least
one instant's clear immortality, let us at least record her
name, which happened to be Enid Hofstatter.

"I hate to sound like a nut," Vicky Kinian said in a low
voice, "but I can't get over the feeling that somebody's
watching me whenever I come in this place."

Enid, who was not going to Europe or anywhere else,
and who on this day of Vicky's initiation into the Jet Set
was on the verge of strangling on her own envy, blinked
at her through smartly framed glasses.

"So what? Probably some handsome hunk of man has already spotted you as a fellow passenger and can't wait till
you're on the plane together. Is that *bad?*"

Vicky showed with her grimace that she did consider it
bad. Like most young women, from Los Angeles to the
Eastern Marches, she harbored the deep suspicion that
her hometown was inhabitated by the most boring spec-
imens of masculinity on earth.

Within five minutes she had added the stapled booklet of tickets to the other vital papers in her purse. Then
as she thanked the travel agent and turned away from the
counter she was once more so overwhelmed by the sensation that she was being spied on that she swept her eyes
over the entire room in the hope of spotting her phantom
shadow. But the other customers in the office seemed fully
involved with business of their own. She said nothing to
Enid this time, and tried to convince herself that she had

seen too many old Hitchcock movies on the late late show.

The two girls had scarcely left the place when a tall man in an inconspicuous blue suit stepped from the doorway of a store opposite, quickly crossed the street, and entered the same travel agency.

As he approached the counter the manager noticed him and raised a hand.

"Ah, Mr Jaeger!" The travel agent paused and glanced around the room, then leaned forward across the counter and held down his voice. "Miss Kinian was just here, getting her ticket."

The tall man smiled. His smile, momentarily tempering the sharp line of a broad thin-lipped mouth, was more aggressive than charming—the kind of smile an ambitious executive might give to a subordinate. A fierce purposefulness was stamped in his sharp features and bluish-green eyes and reflected even in the closely cropped hair, which had once been a light blond and now, tempered with grey, was like polished steel.

"I know," he said. "I deliberately avoided her so that she can be completely surprised. You have my ticket?"

His words were precise and clipped, with a trace of an accent which any American would have vaguely assumed was regional rather than foreign.

"Here you are," the manager answered, producing a folder. "Flight 624 to Lisbon via New York."

Jaeger took the multiple ticket from the man and flipped through its thin sheaf of leaves.

"And my seat is definitely next to Miss Kinian's on the transatlantic leg of the flight?"

"Yes sir. The young lady should be bowled over when her godfather shows up right next to her. How long *is* it since you last met her?"

The customer tucked his ticket into his jacket pocket and returned the travel agent's professional smile.

"Not since she was a tiny little girl," he said. "But I was very close to her father. Until he died, you would have called us inseparable."

If he had been as nervous or as sensitive as Vicky Kinian, he would have had the same psychic impression of being followed, and he would have been just as right. He would also have been thoroughly capable of doing something about it. But unfortunately for him, he was so preoccupied with his own pursuit that he never noticed the elderly gentleman with the white Vandyke whiskers and old-fashioned pince-nez, leaning on a heavy cane at the window of an adjacent bookshop, who turned slightly to observe his departure, looking rather like a benevolent Trotsky.

For Vicky Kinian, the first part of her trip, including a hectic sightseeing stopover in New York City, had been such a frenzied medley of re-claiming and re-registering baggage, of transfers between ramps and gates and buses and airports and hotel and taxis, that she was already in a state of somewhat dazed exhaustion when she emerged from the last human maelstrom of Kennedy Airport's waiting rooms and once more entered the clean cool hyperinsulated interior of a jet primed for the takeoff for Lisbon, and perhaps the first answer to a mystery that had obsessed her all her life. She stepped into the pale blue tunnel of the plane's fuselage prepared to collapse in her assigned seat and thank the fates for letting her be born in the wide smog-free spaces of the American Midwest.

"Vicky Kinian!"

The sound of her own name was so unexpected that for a couple of seconds it meant no more to her than the bump of a piece of hand luggage on the floor of the plane.

"Vicky! Is it really you?"

She stared at the platinum-haired stewardess in the neat

grey uniform who was speaking to her, and then she and the other girl laughed with amazement.

"Freda Oliveiros! Who would've thought we'd have a class reunion like this?"

The stewardess, pretty in a brittle and slightly hard-featured way, led her down the aisle, talking all the time.

"Not me. I never did go much for that old-school-garter bit. But it's good to see that you've made the grade—a cash customer on a flight like this!"

"Don't be silly! I work in a filing-cabinet prison a lot harder than you do on this gorgeous thing. I just . . ."

Freda Oliveiros got a dirty look from her co-stewardess as a sudden influx of passengers began to clog the plane's entrance.

"You'll have to tell me all about it later, Vicky. Here's your seat. I'll drop by as soon as I can take a breath."

Vicky's seat was on the aisle. The place next to the window was already taken by a light-haired man in a blue suit. He gave her a pleasant nod as she sat down but did not say anything. She was glad of that. She had dreaded the possibility of spending eight hours or so as captive audience of some dimwit whose conversational kindling had been collected from the pages of a fifty-cent joke book.

Flight phobia returned briefly as the big jet lumbered through takeoff. Once it was safely airborne, Vicky's fear evaporated, but her hands were still unconsciously gripping the armrests on either side of her seat so tightly that her knuckles were blotchy white. The man next to her noticed and she quickly loosened her fingers.

"Quite right," her companion said in a cultivated, faintly accented voice. "I think the plane can stay up without our help now."

For some reason his thin-lipped smile, showing teeth that were almost too white and perfect, disconcerted her.

"I needn't pretend I'm not a coward about this," she said

with a nervous laugh. "This is only the second time I've ever been off the ground."

Vicky had half-expected everybody on the plane except herself to be at the very least a film star or a millionaire playboy. This man was no movie star she had ever seen, and something told her that he was no playboy either. Her imagination, working on his sharp tanned face and calculating narrow eyes, pictured him as the chief of some construction firm in the Middle East, or an oil geologist from Venezuela. What he confessed to her did much less to enliven her dreams.

"Don't worry about being uneasy," he said. "I fly constantly, and I still don't believe these monsters can get off the ground. Let me introduce myself. I'm Curt Jaeger, a salesman of watches."

"I'm Vicky Kinian, a bookkeeper."

Curt Jaeger began asking all the conventional polite questions and, in answer to hers, told her about his life as a commercial traveller between Switzerland and North America, with occasional side trips to Brazil and Portugal.

"What a wonderful life," Vicky sighed. "I've never even been out of America before."

"But now you are going as a tourist, for pleasure, which is more than I can say," Jaeger answered. "Tell me about your plans."

He had a quiet way of inspiring confidence, but not enough to make Vicky confess to anything more than a sightseer's interest in Europe. She enjoyed talking to him, though, and was almost disappointed when, during their early dinner, he left most of his food on his tray and swallowed two small pills.

"I'm afraid you will have to excuse me," he told her. "I am always so afraid of airsickness that I can never enjoy the food on these trips. The best condition for me now is to be asleep."

"I'm sorry. I never realized . . ."

"Nothing to worry about. I'll be dead to the world inside of ten minutes. And if you don't mind some advice from a traveller much more experienced than he likes to admit, get some sleep yourself. In the morning I'd enjoy giving you a few suggestions about what you should see in Lisbon."

"I'd appreciate that," she said. "I hope you feel better."

"I will," he said drowsily, and mumbled an indistinct goodnight as he turned his back towards her and settled his head on a pillow next to the window.

Many of the other passengers were settling down for the short night as their dinner trays were taken away. The cabin lights dimmed, and Vicky began to think of sleep herself.

"Hi, globetrotter," said a low, cheerful voice. "Shall we talk a bit now?"

It was Freda Oliveiros, trim and still unwilted.

"Wonderful," said Vicky. "I can't get over running into you here."

Freda perched on the arm of Vicky's seat and kept her conversation down to a loud whisper.

"Who'd have thought it, Vicky! From that little school in Dullsville, me a flying waitress, and you part of the carriage trade."

"If I'd had to spend another uninterrupted summer holding hands with an adding machine I'd have been completely off my rocker," Vicky confessed. "So I decided to go for broke—and I do mean broke! I'm splurging a few bucks my father left me for me twenty-fifth birthday, and I couldn't think of a better way to do it than seeing some of the places where he was during the war."

"That's right," Freda said, "your dad was a spy, wasn't he? Made you quite an exotic character back at Myrtle Hill."

"German measles would've seemed exotic at Myrtle Hill," Vicky replied. "But now that you mention it, there is a little more to this trip than . . ."

She stopped and compressed her lips. She had blurted out the words without thinking, mostly from a desire to impress an old-time confidante, and maybe to get the burden of the secret off her mind. Now Freda, sensing a confession in the offing, pounced.

"What? Don't tell me you've taken up the cloak-and-dagger racket too?"

Vicky glanced at Curt Jaeger's back; the rhythm of his breathing was slow and deep. The middle-aged man and woman on the other side of the aisle were engaged in their own low-voice conversation. Ahead of them she could see the broad gleaming dome of a baldheaded man with a hearing-aid bent close over a magazine.

"Promise you won't tell anybody?" she asked Freda.

"Cross my heart."

"Well," Vicky whispered, "my father wrote a letter from Lisbon just before he disappeared and sent it to a lawyer in Des Moines, but the lawyer wasn't to let me have it until I was twenty-five, assuming my father hadn't come back by then. He gave it to me on my birthday."

"And?"

"It was very peculiar, as if my father couldn't really say what he meant. After all those years . . . he just said he hoped I'd come to Lisbon . . ."

"Sort of a slightly overdue wish-you-were-here?" prompted Freda.

"And he . . . he told me something to do when I got there."

Freda waited until she could stand the silence no longer.

"For Pete's sake, what? You've got *me* hooked now!"

Vicky looked around uneasily.

"I . . . I don't want to say any more now," she said. "But I can tell you that until I've done that first thing he asked me to do, the whole business is as much a mystery to me as it is to you."

One of the other stewardesses came down the aisle and muttered to Freda "You're wanted up front," before she continued on.

"Just a sec," Freda said, and turned back to Vicky. "This sounds more intriguing all the time. So it really *is* Kinian, the international private eye-full."

"It probably won't turn out to amount to anything," Vicky said. "I know I sound silly, and I shouldn't have bored you with it."

"That's a laugh. I really *do* happen to be the maddest spy-story fan on either side of this ocean. And I've also had a bit of experience finding my way around Lisbon—especially alone in the wee hours when some magnate got too big for his girdle. Maybe I'll be able to help you. I've got a two-day layover there." She got to her feet. "If I don't want to be stranded there, permanently, I'd better get back to my job. Sorry I've got to run. Catch a few winks and I'll see you in the morning."

Vicky thought she could go to sleep now. There was something about sharing almost anything that made it easier to live with. But in this case, if she could have known just how generously she had shared her story the effect on her would have been anything but relaxing.

Curt Jaeger's thin lips, pressed close against his pillow, wore the faintest twist of a smirk. For the first time since finishing his dinner he allowed himself to think of going to sleep.

And two seats ahead, on the opposite side of the aisle, the baldheaded man with the white goatee and pince-nez, under cover of his magazine, slipped a curiously oversized hearing-aid microphone and amplifier unit into his coat pocket and switched off its battery.

3

Morning on the jetliner was so short and so crammed with facewashing, hairbrushing, and mass-produced breakfasts that there was only space for the shortest snatches of conversation. Vicky and Curt Jaeger, mopping up the last of their scrambled eggs, discovered they were both staying at the same hotel.

"Both of us at the Tagus!" Jaeger said. "Really? What a delightful coincidence. Now it doesn't matter so much that I've not had time to give you my tips on Lisbon. I'll be there myself for a few days and maybe you'll even let me give you a guided tour in person . . ."

"I couldn't put you to so much trouble," Vicky said without even trying to sound as if she meant it.

Jaeger laughed.

"I'd hardly consider it trouble. When you've had time to catch your breath we'll make a plan. Right now we'd better fasten our safety belts."

When the plane had landed, the state of semi-suspended animation in which the passengers had spent most of the flight was changed to a rush of activity. With raincoats over arms and small baggage in hand they filed down the gangway into the blinding furnace of a Portuguese summer's morning. Freda Oliveiros, saying conventional farewells to the travellers as they disembarked, had just time to give Vicky an encouraging pat on the arm and speak a few private words.

"I'll meet you at your hotel as soon as I've changed into my civvies, okay? Which is it?"

"The Tagus. Couldn't you stay with me there?"

"Thanks, but the airline keeps a couple of apartments in town for holdover crews, and I've got some clothes there.

It doesn't cost a centavo, so why make your bill any bigger? I'll just pop over to your place soon."

"Great," Vicky agreed, and hurried on down the steps and across the hot pavement to the arrival portals.

Curt Jaeger, ahead of her in the immigration line, gave up his place and joined her as they, with their fellow-passengers, filed respectfully past the uniformed inspectors to have their passports stamped. This internationally idiotic ritual, followed by the no less universally pointless struggle through a perfunctory Customs checkpoint, actually introduced only a very moderate delay before Vicky and her self-appointed protector were standing on the curb outside the terminal's main entrance. It was only natural that they should share a taxi to their hotel, but Vicky felt worried about obligating herself to Jaeger. He had already tipped the porters who had carried out their luggage.

"If we're going to be doing some of the same things, like this," she said, "I really can't let you pay. Here . . . for the porters."

She thrust out a palmful of Portuguese coins that she had just obtained at the airport *casa de câmbio,* and with an indulgently amused look he chose a few escudos.

"Very well, Miss Kinian, we shall keep this all very Dutch, within limits, but let me explain to you that I am on an expense account—and expense accounts, like justice, are quite blind. Or perhaps I should say, like dead men they tell no tales."

His choice of simile seemed peculiarly unapt to Vicky, but she reminded herself that there was no way he could have known how they applied bizarrely to her own situation. She settled back and began to enjoy the indescribable excitement of knowing that she, Vicky Kinian the nobody, was for the first time in her life on foreign soil.

The taxi was soon entering the outskirts of the city, and when she leaned her head near the window on her side

she could watch a fast-changing prospect of small busy shops,
tree-lined walks, and above on the steep hillsides clusters
and rows of colourwashed houses—pink, yellow, and green
—baking like festive cakes in the sun.

"It's beautiful!" she exclaimed.

"Maybe you'd like to see more, then," Jaeger suggested.
He leaned forward and spoke to the driver in Portuguese.
"I've asked him to take us the long way around, by the
waterfront," he explained.

The cab followed a street which led down a valley towards the sea-like estuary of the River Tagus on which the
city faces. The efficient plainness of modern commercial
buildings was occasionally relieved by such a startling souvenir of gaudy Moorish extravagance that Vicky's head was
constantly kept bobbing from one side to the other.

"This stewardess on the flight," Jaeger said, "is she a good
friend of yours?"

He spoke almost too casually, but Vicky was in no frame
of mind to detect subtleties of tone.

"Oh, Freda?" she said. "We were in school together when
we were teen-agers, but I haven't seen her since—until last
night. She knows Lisbon quite well, of course. I'm lucky to
have run into her."

She did not take her eyes off the new views of pastel
houses, water and cliffs that the taxi's route opened to her.
She was sure she had never been more thrilled in her life,
and she did not think of the implications of what she had
said until Jaeger spoke again.

"I hope that doesn't mean I shall lose the privilege of
helping you to enjoy Lisbon a little myself."

Vicky turned with a quick apologetic smile.

"Of course not! I'm very lucky to have run into you, too,
and I appreciate—"

He raised a hand to stop her.

"You have nothing to appreciate yet. Maybe a division

of labor is the best solution, since you're so popular. Your old school friend can guide you for the day while I make my business calls, but would you give me the pleasure of taking you to dinner tonight? As a professional salesman, I can offer the inducement that in these Catholic countries bars and restaurants don't always welcome a woman alone."

She had already thought of that.

"Well, thank you. I'd love to." Then she thought of something else. "Oh, dear!"

"Is something wrong?" her companion asked.

"Well, I was just thinking. If I go with Freda during the day and then go out with you in the evening it might seem as if I was just making use of her and then leaving her on her own."

Jaeger deliberated for just a few seconds, looking ahead over the taxi driver's shoulder.

"I agree," he said at length. "That would not be nice, so by all means let her come with us. Let her show you inside the churches and shops. I think I can be a better guide to a good dinner, and I should be happy to have you both as my guests."

Although that was what she had wanted him to say, Vicky had to make a perfunctory protest, but he interrupted after her first word.

"Remember," he said, "the expense account."

She laughed.

"All right. You win. You've got yourself a date with a couple of jabbering American females. I hope you won't be sorry."

"I think I can promise you," Jaeger said smoothly, "that I won't be."

Their circuit of Lisbon's waterfront and center seemed finished so soon that Vicky was amazed when she looked at her watch and realized that it had been almost an hour since they had left the airport.

"I'd better get on to the hotel," she said reluctantly.
"Freda is supposed to meet me there, and she may beat me
to it at this rate."

"Don't worry," said Jaeger. "We're almost there now,
and I won't delay you any more. I'll call for you and your
friend at seven o'clock this evening."

As soon as they arrived and registered at the Hotel Tagus
—whose relationship to Lisbon's River Tagus existed more
in its christener's imagination than in geographical fact—
Vicky had thanked Jaeger and gone straight to her room.
It was larger than she had expected, and because of its
thick outer walls was as cool as a limestone cave. A small
private balcony—there was one for every room in the four-
storey building—looked from her third-floor vantage point
out over the red-tiled roofs and peacefully tinted walls
that sloped away towards the distant bright blue of the
estuary.

After enjoying the view for a minute she stepped back
inside the room, closed the French doors behind her,
loosened her dress, and started unpacking her suitcases. It
was good to be alone for the first time in many hours.

She would have taken considerably less pleasure in her
apparent solitude, and her room's old-fashioned spacious-
ness and agreeable temperature, if she had known that her
neighbour on the right-hand side as she faced the estuary
had been either listening to or watching every move she
made since the bellhop who had brought her luggage upstairs had closed her door behind him. She would have been
even more troubled if she had recognized him as the same
bald stout man with the hearing-aid who had been a fellow-
passenger on the flight from New York.

Now he sat in his own room, with his short legs propped
up quite comfortably, as if he had been doing this sort of
thing all his life—which he had—stroking his white Vandyke beard and letting a pair of ingenious mechanical con-

trivances do most of the work of eavesdropping for him. When Vicky had been on her balcony he had been able, while sitting just inside the doors leading to his own balcony, to see every move she made in the angled mirror of a periscope-like device attached to an extension of his walking stick. Then, when she had gone back into her room, he had turned his attention to the amplifier of his kingsized hearing-aid. A wire from the flat metal box led to a plug in his ear, bringing him the sound of even the most lady-like cough or discreet footstep from the other side of the wall.

For a short while he heard little more than footsteps. Then there were the relatively explosive sounds of a door opening and the eruption of female conversation. The first voice was not that of Vicky Kinian.

"Here I am, ready or not!"

Vicky Kinian's words were slower paced and softer than her visitor's.

"Good heavens, Freda, I don't know how you did it. You look straight out of *Vogue*, and I still feel as if I'd just spent three days on a roller-coaster."

The next few minutes of feminine chitchat held no special interest for him. He sat like a bored television viewer waiting for the "station identification" commercials to get off his screen, until the next-door conversation had turned to something less cosmically inane.

"I can line up dates for both of us if you're interested," the visitor—whose voice he recognized having heard on the plane the night before—was saying. "But I suppose you're too wrapped up in your private scavenger hunt to care about a couple of mere cork ranchers."

"Well, my scavenger hunt is the main thing I'm interested in at the moment, but I beat you to it in the date department: I've already got one for both of us—if *you're* interested!"

"Good grief, a faster worker than Oliveiros!" the other

girl exclaimed. "I knew I was slipping, but maybe I'd better rush for the altar before it's too late. Who are the lucky guys?"

"It's just one lucky guy," Vicky Kinian said. "That man who sat next to me on the plane—Mr Jaeger. He invited us both to dinner."

"Right. I remember: tall, blond, and foxy. He seemed nice enough, and who are we to turn down a free meal?"

The question seemed to be settled, and the listener's experienced ears detected that both women were now on their feet.

"Well," the visitor said, "what does your father's letter want you to see first?"

Vicky Kinian read in a nervous, almost awed voice, picking her way carefully over the Portuguese words that were interspersed with the English.

"In Lisbon, go to Segurança's Antique Shop on Rua De Ouro at the corner of Viseli. They will remember me. Ask for the little box I paid a deposit on."

"And?" the other girl asked.

"That's all. He doesn't explain."

"Well, that must be one humdinger of a box to be worth all this trouble . . . or else it must have something pretty fancy in it."

"Do you know where this place is?" Vicky Kinian asked.

"I thought I knew every antique shop in Lisbon, but that's a new one on me. I can lead you to the spot with no trouble, though. Let's go have a look-see."

The goateed man had listened to the parting close of the door, placed his hearing-aid in his jacket pocket, and made a few notes on a small pad. Then he had hauled in his cane, slipped off its contrivance of angled mirrors, telescoped it back to its normal length, put on his hat, and set out for a bit of sightseeing in the vicinity of Rua De Ouro and Viseli.

4

Vicky Kinian and Freda Oliveiros stepped out of their taxi
on to a sidewalk bordering a broad uncrowded intersection.
During the ride from the hotel they had chattered about
everything under the sun except the riddle they were on
their way to solve, and now that they were brought face-
to-face with the question mark they seemed to have nothing to say at all. Standing in the cool shadow of a large tree
they let their eyes survey the complete three hundred and
sixty degrees of the panorama. To the left was a café—
round wrought-iron tables in the open air beneath a blue
and yellow awning. Opposite where they stood was an
apartment house, and then an office building of some kind.
To their right was a bank. Behind them was a park.

"Something must be wrong," Vicky said. "Are you sure
this is the right corner?"

"Check your letter again."

Vicky confirmed the address: Segurança's Antique Shop
on Rua De Ouro at the corner of Viseli.

"Well, there's the corner, but there isn't any antique
shop," Freda said. "Maybe it went out of business, unless
it's in a back room somewhere. Or maybe . . ."

"Wait a minute," Vicky broke in. "Look at the name on
that bank."

In large letters carved into the stone pediment above
the bank's columned entrance were the words, *BANCO
ANTIGO DE SEGURANÇA.*

"*Segurança,*" Vicky read carefully. "It's the same word."

"And *antigo,*" Freda carried on. "There's your 'antique'
shop all right. *Segurança* means something like 'security'."

Vicky was frowning as she glanced from the letter to
the marble portico of the bank.

"But if it's the bank why didn't he just say so? Now that we've seen what he meant, it sounds like something out of a mystery story."

"Well, at least we've solved the first clue," Freda said cheerfully.

"We just followed his directions, but I'd hardly say we'd found any answers," Vicky rejoined. "Why be so cryptic about a perfectly respectable-looking bank?"

"Search me, Vicky. But let's face it—nothing about this whole deal is exactly on the up-and-up, or your father would just have left you a nice traditional will to his estates and acres, not to mention his millions."

They were walking almost cautiously towards the bank as they talked. Vicky felt a strange reluctance to get too near the place. Somehow its marble massiveness reminded her of a mausoleum.

"He never had acres or millions," she said. "He hardly even had thousands."

"Well," said Freda, "if you'll excuse my delicacy, let's be charitable and assume dear old dad handled things this way because he was in the cloak-and-dagger business and not because he was some kind of a nut. How does that letter go on?"

"They will remember me. Ask for the little box I paid a deposit on."

They were at the foot of the wide stone stairway leading into the bank. Simultaneously they both stopped and exchanged looks of sudden realization.

"A safe deposit box!" they said almost simultaneously.

"Things are looking up, girl!" continued Freda. "Let's go."

They climbed the steps quickly and walked into the bank's ornate cavernous main floor. Vicky questioned a woman at the first barred window. She was asked, in hesitant English, to wait. A few moments later an old man with rimless round spectacles perched on his pointed beak walked stiffly across the tiled floor to meet them. Against the background of bars and barrel-vaulted stone ceiling he looked very appropriately like some gnomish custodian of long-interred wealth.

"*Senhorita*," he said as Vicky stepped towards him. "I am Valdez, Assistant Manager. May I help you? I am told it is a matter which goes back many years, and I am most qualified on such matters."

If he smiled, the event was obscured by a hanging garden of white moustache which covered his mouth entirely except for a bit of central lower lip.

"I've come to ask about a safe deposit box my father rented here in 1945," Vicky told him. "His name was Kinian—Major Robert Kinian."

Assistant Manager Valdez squinted briefly and shook his head.

"I do not remember him myself, *senhorita*, but it is easy to look him up. Come into my office, please."

He led the way with a stiff-legged brisk gait to a private office rich in waxed wood and leather. Vicky gave more details. Shortly Valdez sat at his massive desk and opened a bound volume of records with the date 1945–46 on its spine. As he was going over one of the pages with a magnifying glass Freda made a *sotto voce* comment to Vicky, who was sitting next to her in a huge wooden chair.

"If George Washington ever banked here, I bet this place would still have *his* checks."

"*Senhorita*," said Valdez unexpectedly without looking up from his magnifying glass, "this bank still holds an unpaid note signed by Christopher Columbus."

Again, if the Assistant Manager's drollery was accompanied by any trace of a smile, he was the only one who could have known it, and Vicky and Freda glanced at one another like two schoolgirls trying to stifle giggles.

"Ah!" said Valdez suddenly, "here is the name Kinian,

with a special notation. The box was taken by Robert Kinian on February 8, 1945, and the rent paid in advance for thirty years.

When he looked up from the minuscule pen scratches of his ledger Vicky was leaning forward so tensely that he paused and blinked.

"Do not fear, *senhorita*, the box is certain to be here, quite secure. The vault is even safe against earthquakes. We have learned from unhappy experience."

"I wasn't worried about that," Vicky assured him. "I'm just anxious to see the box."

Valdez stood up.

"Good," he said briskly. "All that is needed from you is some identification."

Vicky opened her purse.

"Here's my passport."

"Very good." Valdez took the green booklet and inspected its first pages. " 'Victoria Eileen Kinian.' Yes, that is correct. I am authorized to give you a key to this box. Now, if you will follow me, please . . ."

They went with him out of the office, across the main floor again, and into a crypt-like stone chamber behind one of the counters. Armed with a ring of jangling keys, Valdez left the girls, shuffled off down a tunnel, and returned after an almost unbearable delay carrying a large metal box in his arms. He put the box on a table in the center of the room, handed Vicky a key, and held a chair for her and then for Freda.

"Regard the box as your own now, *senhorita*," he said. "I shall leave you alone."

"Our own private dungeon," Freda said with a shiver when he had gone, gazing around at the forbidding walls of the room. "Solid granite three feet thick. Open that thing and let's get out of here. What are you waiting for?"

Vicky was sitting with the key in her hand, hesitating

to use it. Freda's question broke the spell, and she inserted the key carefully into the lock at the end of the box.

"I don't know," she confessed. "For some reason, this is all giving me the creeps. I feel a little like—who was that girl in the old story who opened a box and discovered too late what she'd let out?" She turned the key. "Pandora," she remembered aloud. "Pandora."

The only sound in the bank's inner sanctum was the faintly echoing click of a lock which had not been used for twenty-five years. Vicky touched the cold metal cover of the container as though it might give her an electric shock and then lifted it.

Looking very much alone on the bottom of the box was a white envelope, slightly yellowed with age like the letter that the lawyer had given her in Iowa.

"It doesn't seem like much," she said huskily.

She was staring down at it without showing any sign of intending to pick it up.

"Well, for goodness' sake, it's not going to bite you!" Freda encouraged her.

Vicky finally reached in and lifted it out. It was somewhat bulkier than she had thought at first glance.

"I think it's just a letter," she said appraisingly.

Freda sat back with a shake of her platinum-blond head.

"Your old man must've eaten wild goose every day and twice on Sundays. Okay, read us the next installment."

Vicky had started to tear open the envelope, but then she stopped, weighing it in her palm.

"I'd rather not—here," she said. "This feels like a regular project. Let's go back to my room where we can settle down —in case there's a shock that's going to knock me flat."

Freda stood up with a shrug of suffering resignation.

"It's your snipe hunt, sweety. My lot is but to follow and hope you drop a few golden crumbs when you finally hit

the jackpot. The prize must be pretty big if it was worth
putting up this much of a smokescreen to cover it."

They left Senhor Valdez with thanks and an empty
coffer, and took a taxi back to the Tagus Hotel. Vicky was
subdued during the drive and avoided saying a word about
her father or the trail he had left behind him. Outside the
quiet entrance of the hotel, which seemed almost completely deserted in comparison with its more typically central hostelries, Freda stopped and held Vicky back.

"I know all this is none of my business," she said. "My
only excuse is that *you* got me hooked on this awful suspense. I won't come in if you don't want me to."

"Of course you should come in!" Vicky shook herself out
of her abstracted state enough to put some sincere warmth
into her answer. "I got you interested in this, and I might
never even have found that bank without you. Let's get
upstairs and have a look."

They walked into the low-keyed interior of the Tagus's
lobby, past potted palms and overstuffed sofas. Freda, taking everything in like a nervous bird as usual, focussed on
the reception desk and nudged Vicky.

"Half-step, comrade," she whispered. "Dig the gorgeous
chunk of *senhor*."

Vicky looked, and as she did so the tall blackhaired man
who had been talking to the receptionist happened to glance
up and look right at her. He was so unbelievably handsome, so easily and effortlessly elegant, and carried such
magnetism in his steady gaze that she felt a quick shiver
pass completely through her body.

"With those blue eyes I don't think he's a *senhor*," she
muttered inadequately.

"I may fight you for him," Freda rejoined under her
breath. "He's the best-looking devil I've seen in ages."

Vicky peeked back over her shoulder at the cleanly honed
hawkish profile as she climbed the stairs.

"Oh well," she sighed, "why fight? We'll never see him again anyway."

Everyone who has ever read any other story about Simon Templar, alias the Saint, will infallibly identify that as one of the most hard-worked errors of prophecy in the Saga. But this chronicler cannot fiddle with the record merely to avert a cliché.

That's what the girl said. Honestly.

II: How Freda Oliveiros shared a
    Taxi, and Curt Jaeger's appetite
    was Strained.

Without even waiting to open his suitcase, once he had seen it deposited in his room and taken possession of his key, Curt Jaeger had left the hotel again and completed a swift and efficient rendezvous with a business associate of long standing, whose interest in Swiss watches was basically limited to those that he fancied to wear himself, and those that in commercially viable quantities might be smuggled or stolen for sale in some underground market.

What this invaluable local contact really specialized in was methods of population control which are viewed by the temperal powers of Portugal with as much disfavour as they are by the Vatican, since they do not go to work until many years after the critical instant of conception. But on order, and against sufficient cash payment, this unobtrusive handyman could guarantee the removal, permanent or temporary, of unwelcome members from one's circle of acquaintance. His professional name was simply Pedro; he was small as a jockey, and he had the black blinking eyes of a myopic rat.

He watched with Jaeger from one of the outdoor tables of a café down the street as Freda and Vicky returned to the Tagus after their trip to the bank. Pedro's unlovely facial structure was overhung by a nose of stunning amplitude shaped like a headsman's axe. In the shadows of this massive outcropping dwelt a pencil-thin moustache which jutted on either side directly out from its moorings to quiver its tips just beyond its cultivator's high cheekbones. When Pedro squinted at the two American girls as they walked from their taxi into the hotel, his Stygian eyes blinked more rapidly than usual down the slopes of his nose, and his pilous antennae vibrated like the feelers of a roach sensing feasts beneath the kitchen sink.

"The dark one is prettier, but the blond one did not look so bad either," he said in hissing Portuguese. "It seems a pity you cannot . . . avoid her in some other way."

"I am not hiring you to think for me, Pedro," Jaeger retorted. "I am hiring you to do two things, and to do them quickly and efficiently. Get the blonde out of the way immediately, and before you dispose of her learn all she has been told by the dark girl about letters or other information from the dark girl's father. Is that understood?"

"*Bem*," assented Pedro. "I understand."

Jaeger's hard turquoise eyes were capable of projecting a threat which made even Pedro squirm and nervously suck his two prominent front teeth.

"And if," Jaeger said, "you should get any romantic Latin ideas about keeping her hidden away for yourself, or selling her to Arab slave traders, or some other nonsense, you had better remember . . ."

"*Senhor!*" Pedro interjected, with a look of reproachful innocence.

"You had better remember what happened to Tico," Jaeger concluded.

Pedro looked thoroughly unhappy as he remembered what had happened to Tico those many years ago.

"It shall be as you say," he promised.

"Good. Everything is in order, then? Your friend who drives a taxi, is he ready?"

"He waits just around the corner now."

"Very well. Tell him no more than you have to—and meet me here this evening at six-thirty to let me know what you have learned from the blonde."

"*Bem!*" Pedro said, concluding the consultation. "We shall be waiting to welcome her when she comes out."

Feeling safe at last in her hotel room, all thought of the glamorously Mephistophelean stranger whom she had seen in the lobby passed out of her mind for the moment as she hurried to open her father's delayed-action envelope. She almost dropped her purse in her eagerness to get the envelope out of it, but then she hesitated before tearing the sealed paper; in spite of her feverish curiosity she would almost have preferred that a ghostly wind would tear the missive out of the fingers and whip it out of the window.

"Just let me read it to myself first," she said to Freda. "Then if I can tell you all about it, I will."

"If you don't mind I'll take the strain off my stays in the meantime," Freda said accommodatingly.

She spread herself out in an easy chair as Vicky tore open the envelope. Inside were six hand-written pages.

Still standing, Vicky unfolded them, and as she read her anxious expression turned to one of amazed shock. She sank slowly to a sitting position on the edge of the bed as she read on.

At long last she mumbled: "This is fantastic . . ."

Freda could control herself no longer.

"*What* is, Vicky, for heaven's sake?"

Vicky skimmed quickly through the last two pages before answering. Then, her face drained of colour, she clutched the disordered leaves of the letter in her hands and stared dizzily out at the sky.

"I can't tell you, Freda," she said in a trance-like monotone. "At least, not now."

Freda stood up. Determined good humour veneered a note of understandable disappointment when she replied.

"I shouldn't be here now anyway. I should have kept my long nose out of your private affairs in the first place."

Vicky, realizing that she could not possibly tell Freda what the letter said, pretended to be more badly shaken than she was.

"Please forgive me, Freda," she breathed. "But I've got to think it out before I can talk about it."

Freda had recovered, at least superficially, all of her usual bounce.

"Forget it, honey! I'll go take me a siesta at the communal pad and be back for our dinner date. How's that?"

"Fine. I'm so sorry, but you can't imagine what a shock I've had."

"Don't worry your pretty little bean about me. Get some rest yourself, and I'll join you at seven."

"Thanks so much."

Freda turned back from the doorway and said: "I just hope *my* father never writes me a cliff-hanging letter like that!"

For a second or two she hesitated in the corridor, turning over the idea of going back into the room and cancelling out the three-cornered evening with Vicky and Curt Jaeger, which promised to be about as titillating as last night's lettuce salad. She was slightly irritated already to have wasted half a day for nothing but a quick brushoff when Vicky finally found her goodies. But her alternatives in evening revelry happened to be fairly uninspiring—and besides, plain old-fashioned nosiness made her want to drag out the class reunion bit until she had been let in on Vicky's secret.

She was turning away from Vicky's room when she noticed that the door of the room opposite was ajar. Through the opening she caught just a glimpse of the breathtakingly handsome dark-haired man she had spotted beside the reception desk a few minutes before. She slowed her pace hopefully, but he seemed not to have seen her, and the door closed. That, apparently, was going to be typical of her luck on this particular Lisbon layover. With a philosophical jerk of her shoulders, she walked briskly away to the stairs.

If she had dreamed how strongly the man called Curt Jaeger shared her lack of enthusiasm for a triangular dinner date, and to what extremes he had already gone to ensure the reduction of the company to a more intimate number, the last thing she would ever have willingly done was to walk down the steps of the Tagus Hotel, but she was not a morbidly hyper-imaginative type. Although the Tagus was not the sort of place that ambitious cabmen would choose as a waiting post, she felt no suspicion at seeing one parked in the street. She assumed that a small man with the large nose and bristling black moustache, his face shadowed by a ludicrously broad-brimmed hat, had just paid the taxi driver for his own ride and that he now bustled to open the door of the car for her out of pure Latin gallantry.

"*Senhorita*," he hissed with a bow as she stepped into the back seat of the automobile.

Then, when she was seated, he suddenly hopped in beside her and slammed the door shut. Instantly the driver pulled away from the curb so fast that she was bounced back against the upholstery.

"Be quiet, *senhorita*, and there weel be no trouble!" the little man said in English.

Freda, who had held her own against considerably more

hefty males than this one, was more angry than scared. She got her purse on her safer side and slid over against the door.

"That's what you think, buster!" she snapped. "Now get out of here pronto or you'll see plenty of trouble! Driver—"

Her uninvited fellow traveller moved so swiftly that she was not sure whether the knife had been whipped from his pocket or whether it had been in his hand all the time. In any case, it was one of those very large switch knives whose butcher-shop blade stays concealed in its weighty handle until a button is pressed. The sharp silvery point flashed out at her like the head of a snake and stopped just short of her ribs.

"Do not waste your voice," the little man said. "The driver weel only pay attention to me. I am suggest that you should pay attention to this that I am holding in my hand."

He nuzzled the point of the blade almost affectionately against the thin material of her dress just below her breast.

"I'll scream my head off," she threatened with less assurance.

"And I would cut your head off and you would not scream any more."

The man seemed to think his rejoinder was humorous, but the sharp tip of his knife pressed harder against her and assured Freda that his basic intentions were entirely serious. She was really terrified for the first time. The driver —the back view of his head reminded her grotesquely of a carved coconut with a cap on—swung his taxi around several corners and headed away from the center of the city. The neighbourhoods they passed through began to deteriorate into jumbles of warehouses, dingy-looking bars, and grubby housing.

"What do you want?" Freda asked tensely. "Where do you think you're taking me?"

"You weel know quick," was the answer. "Do not make trouble."

The cab pulled into a narrow cobbled street of two-storey houses whose walls and window shutters seemed to be nearing the end of an ancient contest to decide which could flake off the most paint or plaster. Freda was so terrified by now that she took in only the vaguest impression of her surroundings. The man with the knife muttered his instructions as the driver opened the door on her side of the automobile.

"You weel get out, please, and go into that house— weethout no fuss!"

The switchblade reinforced his order, and the girl obeyed, clutching her purse tightly against her body almost as if she hoped it was all the men were really after. The car was parked within three paces of a doorway which the driver, in a parody of politeness, held open for her. He was an imbecilic-looking lout with a battered nose and cavernous bushy-browed eye sockets, one of the ugliest mortals she had ever laid eyes on. Even so, she thought she preferred him to the sinister little cutthroat behind her. As she entered the house she looked longingly back over her shoulder past the knifeman's broad-brimmed hat at the sunlight on the wall opposite—and the last thing she saw was the long taxi, black and shining like a well-kept hearse.

The man with the knife locked the door when they were all three inside, and it took several seconds for Freda's eyes to accustom themselves to the dimness of the room. The two windows were shuttered and the driver jerked dusty draperies across them, cutting off the light that would have filtered in through the crevices. The room itself was depressingly shabby and underfurnished, like part of a rental house that had been used by family after family for years until finally it had been closed for months because no one would have it.

"Seet at the table, *senhorita*."

Freda summoned every volt of her courage in a final effort to intimidate her chief captor with sheer defiance.

"You can't get away with this—whatever you think you want! I'm an American citizen, and . . ."

The moustached man's hatchet-chop of a laugh showed just how singularly unimpressed he was by her national prestige and her threats.

"Seet down!" he ordered. "What we want ees so easy, *senhorita*, as you weel see. Do not trouble yourself. Seet at the table—here!"

He kicked a crippled chair into place for her and she sullenly sat on it. The thick wooden slab of a table top in front of her was covered with a film of reddish dust.

"What is it, then?" she demanded.

The driver was standing by as dumb and motionless as a wax-museum Neanderthaler. The other man took paper and pen from his pocket and put them down for her to use.

"Seemply a note to your woman friend at the hotel, to say you have been called away and cannot have dinner tonight."

Freda stared at him with incredulity and the eager hope that she might get out of the situation a lot more easily than she had imagined.

"All this so I'll cancel a dinner date?" she asked.

"*Si, senhorita.* Just write an excuse to your girl friend so her admirer can see her alone."

"Why?"

"I am not like so many questions," the man said more harshly. "Write the letter! Tell her you have business that makes you leave Lisboa."

Freda pondered her situation for just a few seconds, and decided that any further resistance would be a waste of time. She took the pen and wrote a short note in deliberately overformal English saying that she had been called away suddenly to work on a flight.

"Will that do?" she asked curtly, after scrawling her name.

Axe-nose took the piece of paper and scrutinized it word by word. He read it a second time before he nodded.

"Eez okay," he granted.

"I must say Mr Jaeger has a pretty violent way of breaking a date," Freda said. "But now that you've got what he wants, you can let me out of here."

Her kidnapper tucked the note she had written into his jacket. Then, before he answered, he unwrapped, clenched in his teeth, and held a match to a long thin cigar—all with deliberate slowness. The silence was unnerving. The only sound in the thick-walled room was the man's quick sucking of fire into his cheroot. When it was glowing, he snapped the wooden match in half between his fingers and flipped its pieces across the room.

"Oh, no, *senhorita*," he said softly. "I cannot let you out of here. Now that you absence weel be explained—now we can ask you some important questions."

He had put one foot on a rung of her chair and leaned down with his face so close to hers that she could feel the heat of the scarlet glowing coal tip of the cigar which jutted from his mouth.

"But . . ."

She was almost too frightened to say anything, and he cut her off after the first word she uttered. The big knife, which he had kept out of sight while she wrote the letter to Vicky, appeared again from behind his back. He held the blade for her to see.

"No 'but,' *senhorita*," he murmured. "Now you weel answer questions, and you weel answer quickly, or eet weel be a long afternoon that you spend here." He moved the knife towards her midriff until it punctured the thin fabric

of her blouse, and then—like a surgeon beginning to op-
erate—with a slow careful upward movement he slit the
material open all the way to the neckline. "A very long afternoon . . ."

2

Through his half-open door, which gave him an adequately
direct view of the entrance to Vicky Kinian's room across
the hall, Simon Templar had heard Freda's parting line—
"I just hope *my* father never writes me a cliff-hanging letter
like that!"—and had been well aware of her glance into his
room, and of the significant deceleration of her pace as she
passed it. He would have been hardly human, or more like
an authentic saint, if he had not been tempted to accept the
obvious challenge to make a discreet bid for her acquaintance. He could even have twisted the rubber arm of his
conscience with the specious argument that such a ma-
noeuvre would be strictly in the line of duty, anyhow, since
it could be an adroitly indirect way to sneak up on his
prime target. The blonde was not one of the characters of
the script that had been presented to him at the embassy,
but then life almost always ignored the scripts men prepared for it anyway. The important things at the moment
were that Vicky Kinian was in her room and could not get
out without him knowing it, and that with her—unless the
blonde had a more active role than he imagined—was a
fascinating epistle from her departed dad. Whether it was
the same letter she had been given in Iowa or a new one
that had somehow come into her hands in Lisbon did not
make much difference now; in either case it was just the
sort of light reading the Saint craved to while away a few
minutes of his tax-supported holiday in Portugal. And

from that objective he could not let himself for the moment be detoured.

He had gone directly from the American Embassy to the Tagus Hotel after his briefing on the case of the errant Major Kinian, who had somehow neglected to report to his superiors for the past quarter of a century. And as he entered the modest foyer, which was a pleasant but nevertheless gently jolting contrast to those of the chain-store caravanserais to which he had latterly become accustomed, the Saint had been musing on the stupendous changes that had subvened in the two-and-a-half decades since the missing major had last been heard from. That most popular puppet of the newspaper cartoonist, the black octopus with the swastika on its head, had long since withdrawn its tentacles from the borderlands of the abdicated British Empire and disappeared even from children's nightmares. Former heroic allies had become sour antagonists, and one of those which had most cynically played both ends against the middle had spread its web over the world on a scale that made the reach of the black octopus seem puny in comparison.

And yet, through it all, certain denizens of the Pentagon, part of a species which could easily misplace whole shiploads of bulldozer axles and misdirect trainloads of snowboots to Equatorial Africa, had managed to keep a sharp eye out for Major Kinian—and not only that, but also to know when his daughter decided to take her summer holiday. Such atypical cases of bureaucratic alertness were enough to arouse the curiosity of the most skeptical buccaneer—or even of a Saint.

"There is a young American lady staying here whom I would like very much to meet," Simon had said to the desk clerk in clear Portuguese as he took up the pen to sign the register. "Her name is Victoria Kinian."

"Ah, *si*," the clerk said promptly. "She has just arrived this morning."

"*Bem*. But please say nothing to her. There is always a tactful way to arrange these things."

The clerk smiled understandingly, and then came to sudden attention.

"*Senhor!*" he whispered, scarcely moving his lips. "You have good fortune. There comes the lady now. The dark-haired one. The blonde one does not stay here."

At a single glance the Saint had discovered at least one superficial reason why the men of American Intelligence need not have been excessively pitied for the close watch they had kept on Major Kinian's daughter. Unconsciously beautiful in a modest white-and-yellow summer dress, she made her bare-shouldered flashier companion look like the late night shift at a hamburger stand. For just a moment she had met his gaze with interest but without encouragement, and then had turned her head and gone on up the stairs.

"A most lovely young lady," the desk clerk said discreetly.

"Most lovely," Simon agreed. "Have she and her friend been out long?"

"No, *senhor*. Less than two hours."

The Saint thanked him, and followed the bellhop who came to carry his bags. There was no elevator in the building, and they used the same broad stairway which the girls had just climbed.

"*Desculpe-me, faca o favor!*" puffed a voice just behind them, and a small bald roundish man in Vandyke whiskers chugged between Simon and his burdened porter with such urgent speed that he knocked one of the suitcases against the railing. "*Pardon!*" he called back without turning, and bounded out of sight at the top of the stairs like an animated rubber ball.

Pardon, in French pronunciation, being a universal European term of public apology, its use by the bearded man did not give Simon any clue to his nationality, but he made a careful mental note of the stair-hog's personal appearance. It could have been that the man's headlong rush up the steps was due to his being late for an appointment or uncontrollably eager for a cool bath, but it was also just possible that his enthusiasm for climbing was connected with an interest in the comings and going of Vicky Kinian, who had preceded him by just a few minutes. However, there had been no sign of him during the rest of the climb to Simon's room, and the Saint had soon had less remotely speculative things to think about.

Such as the mysterious letter, or letters, upon which Vicky Kinian's enigmatic odyssey seemed to hinge. The immediate problem was to get a look at it, or them, by some means less crude than bursting into the room opposite while the girl was there and hoping to attain his objective by force or menace, with an odds-on risk of hashing up the rest of the game even if that play succeeded. Therefore he would have to wait until she went out—while trying meanwhile to decide whether it would be better to gamble on her having hidden the documents in her room, or having them with her in a purse that might be snatched or rifled somewhere without identifiably involving himself.

It was an exercise in patience which only a most unusual mission could have commanded of him, for the Saint was not by nature a patient man. And it should say enough for the old-time bond between him and the man called Hamilton that he embarked upon it at all.

An hour after the blonde had left, a waiter delivered a tray to the room. Late lunch. Simon followed suit. Then, when long after he had finished his cold chicken and wine nothing more had happened across the hall, he was forced to assume that the lovely object of his watch was taking a siesta—a natural part of the first-day schedule of a transatlantic traveller for whom waking-up time on landing in Portugal would have been three in the morning at home.

Simon, who had flown in the opposite direction, had not

suffered the same bashing of his biological clock, and through plenty of firsthand experience with the relativity of time and space had learned to adapt himself automatically to the most bizarre antics of chronometers and shifting dawns. All the same, a hot afternoon in Lisbon was not ideal for guard duty, and the Saint fought drowsiness as he resigned himself to his vigil.

If he had had any notion of what had happened, and was happening, to Freda Oliveiros, his enforced inaction would have been infinitely harder to endure; but mercifully that knowledge was for ever spared him.

Curt Jaeger, who knew, was emotionally perturbed only by the inevitable native unpunctuality of his temporary deputy. Freshly bathed, shaved, and changed into a newly pressed dark suit, in complete readiness for his date with Vicky Kinian, he was sitting at a table at the café down the street at exactly six twenty-nine. At a quarter to seven he was still nursing a small glass of Robertson's Port and checking his watch every two or three minutes, with progressively increasing irritation. A deadline was rapidly approaching when, through no fault of his own, he could be late to pick up his dinner engagement. Curt Jaeger did not like lateness—his own or other people's—and he sat stiffly, cursing the congenital incompetence of inferior races.

Finally, at almost ten minutes to, Pedro came scurrying around the corner blinking at the red sunset and twitching his thin black antennae. He dropped into a chair opposite Jaeger and began to hiss words so rapidly that even one of his own countrymen might have had trouble understanding him.

"You are late!" Jaeger cut him off. "I always make it a practice to arrive at any appointment at least a minute ahead of time."

Pedro only ducked briefly as if to dodge that bit of uplifting advice, and went on hissing.

"Slow down, at least, so I can understand you!" Jaeger snapped. "Although I have no doubt that what you have to tell me is disappointing."

"The news is bad, *senhor*," Pedro whined.

"Naturally," Jaeger said without emotion. "What did she tell you?"

"Her name—Freda Oliveiros, a stewardess with International Airways. That she was once at school, long ago, with the dark one, Victoria Kinian. But they had not met since, until by chance they were on this flight from New York."

"What else?"

"She could only tell us that the dark one's father had a strong box at the bank. They went to the bank this morning and opened the box and found a letter in it."

Jaeger pushed his port aside and unconsciously tensed forward.

"Well—and what did the letter say?"

"The dark one read it but would not tell the blond one what was in it, except that it seemed very important."

"Idiot!" Jaeger barked. "You believe one girl could keep such a thing from another? You must keep on until you *make* her talk."

Pedro twisted his feet around the legs of his chair and rubbed his hatchet nose with the back of his hand in an embarrassed gesture.

"We tried very hard, until she died," he grumbled. "I think perhaps she truly did not know."

Jaeger had no rebuttal for that. He sat with his jaw clamped shut for a moment while the muscles in his gaunt cheeks worked nervously.

"You tried everything?" he finally asked, wanting to be sure his dissatisfaction was quite clear.

Pedro's black eyes glittered as he remembered some of the things he had done during the long hours of the hot afternoon.

"Everything," he said.

He spoke the word with such evident sincerity that even Jaeger had to be contented.

"So!" he said, slapping the table in front of him with his palms. "That matter is concluded then. I assume you have taken care of the—final details."

Pedro nodded.

"We went by the waterfront on our way here. I have a friend with a trapdoor in the bottom of his boathouse which . . ."

"Never mind telling me the tricks of your filthy trade," Jaeger said coldly. "I am in a hurry. Would you like to earn some more money for an easy job?"

"What is the job?" asked Pedro sensibly.

"I am taking the dark girl out to dinner. When we have left the hotel, go to her room—number 302—and see if you can find the letter they got from the bank."

"*Si*," Pedro said. "I go to the room. But how do I know which is the letter?"

"Bring anything that looks like a letter," Jaeger said impatiently. "Take your time. I shall have the girl out with me for at least two hours from now." He stood up. "But you have made me late and I must go. I can rely on you?"

"*Si!* Room number 302."

"Correct. Telephone me at my room at the Tagus later tonight, and we can arrange a meeting so you can give me what you have found."

"And settle accounts," Pedro said practically.

"Of course," Jaeger replied. "*Até logo.*"

"*Va com Deus*," said Pedro, with no perceptible trace of irony.

His employer did not return the sentiment, but hurried away to keep his appointment with Vicky Kinian. He called her on the house phone, apologized profusely for not being earlier, and tried to compose himself while he waited.

It was now more vital than ever that Major Kinian's daughter should continue to accept him as only a friendly businessman with no more worrisome thought in his head than selling an order of wristwatches or choosing the best wines for dinner.

To Simon Templar, sitting where the open few inches of his door, angled in the dressing-table mirror, were directly in line with the top of the book he was reading, it seemed like a budding eternity before Vicky Kinian finally came out. She looked stunning in a shoulderless black dress and long white gloves, and he briefly wavered again between visiting her empty room, as he had decided, and investigating her in person. But girls going out at the dinner hour in shoulderless black dresses were likely to have plans of their own which would not make them welcome last-minute invitations from total strangers, and furthermore the small beaded bag which he had seen she now carried hardly looked as if it would hold anything momentous in the way of documents. The room was now a more logical and certainly less reckless first possibility to try, and if he drew blank there the alternative would still be open.

He waited until she had had time to get all the way down the stairs. Then he pocketed a small metal implement he had already chosen from a selection in his suitcase after inspecting his own door lock, and armed with this modern open-sesame, prepared to find what treasures or terrors lay hidden in the cave of Major Kinian's disappearance.

3

"It's fortunate there are no cannibals in Lisbon," Curt Jaeger said, coming to meet Vicky as she appeared on the last flight of stairs. "Because, as they say in America, you look good enough to eat. But it's so nice of you to consent to eat with me instead."

He bent to kiss her hand, feeling her fingers tense as he held them, but noting as he straightened up that her cheeks had a pleased glow. She was, in her innocence, as he had assumed, a pushover for what the Americans called the Continental touch. A heavy dose of gallantry with no alarming passes: that should be the most effective formula.

"It's nice of you to invite me," she said, "but I'm afraid that Freda seems to have let us down."

"Perhaps she's expecting us to call for her at her own hotel," he said with a frown of mild concern.

"No. She was supposed to come back at seven, and she hasn't called or anything. I don't understand it."

Jaeger looked around the lobby, and then at the clock behind the desk clerk's counter.

"I'm sorry I am late myself," he said. "I had business at the last minute. Maybe she will show up soon. In the meantime, we could ask if she has sent a message."

They walked to the desk, and in response to Vicky's question the clerk promptly produced an envelope. Before she read the short note inside she glanced at the bottom to confirm that it really was from Freda Oliveiros.

"I don't understand this," she said. "Why ever wouldn't she have phoned me? When did this note come?"

"Half an hour ago, *senhorita*," said the man behind the counter.

"Would she like us to pick her up?" Jaeger asked helpfully.

"No. She says she's been called to replace another stewardess on a flight leaving at once. That was late this afternoon, I guess." Vicky looked up from the paper, her eyes puzzled. "So of course she won't be joining us."

Jaeger shrugged and gestured towards the main exit.

"Well, I am sorry for her, but for myself, this is one case in which a loss is no real loss."

He held the door for her and they walked out on to the tranquil darkening street.

"I just hope you will feel safe with me even though your friend cannot be with us," he said sympathetically.

Vicky was already beginning to cast off any worry she felt about Freda's not showing up.

"Oh, I'm not thinking of that, Mr Jaeger. But I had to disappoint Freda about something earlier today, and I hope she isn't just making an excuse because she's mad at me."

"I'm sure she isn't," Jaeger said with mature assurance. "Now let us eat, drink, and be merry because . . . because that's what one ought to do in Lisbon!"

On that cheerful note he took her away by taxi to one of the golden dining rooms of the Restaurant Avis, and waited until she was semi-steeped in champagne before gently continuing his research into the more secret aspects of her private life.

"I can't help wondering," he began—"Would it be too inquisitive to ask what you did that might have angered your girl friend so much?"

Vicky wished he hadn't brought the subject up again; she had been trying to forget it completely.

"Oh, it was nothing much," she said. "It's hardly worth talking about."

Jaeger sat back in his chair and raised his champagne glass to his lips.

"I see," he said gently. "I thought maybe you were still worrying about it. You looked a thousand miles away."

Vicky realized that she had been staring beyond Jaeger without really seeing anything. She quickly put down her glass and turned all her attention to him.

"I'm so sorry!" she hurried to say. "I suppose there *is* something on my mind, and it *is* tied up with Freda. I might as well tell you, since it's bound to make me act a little funny, and I don't want you to think I'm rude."

"I hope it was nothing so momentous as the fact that both you girls were wearing the same dress when you met to go shopping," Jaeger said with a smile.

Vicky forced herself to laugh and took up her champagne again with relief. She was bursting to share her secrets—and the burden of the tremendous decision her father's second letter asked her to make—just as she had been eager to confide in Freda when they had talked on the plane.

"Nothing as bad as that," she said. She imbibed a large sip from her glass and took the plunge. "It was about a rather mysterious letter that she partly helped me to find. And then when I'd gotten it, I couldn't tell her what was in it. At least I couldn't tell her at the time without thinking it over first. She was hurt, I think—and that was the last I saw of her."

The wine was making her feel more indifferent than disconsolate when she remembered Freda's reaction. She hoped the waiter would bring the Vichyssoise before she started getting dizzy. One cocktail before dinner had always been her limit—and when she had last drunk champagne, at a wedding reception, she had found the whole world swooping and dipping around her head like a carnival run wild.

"This letter—it indeed sounds *very* mysterious," Jaeger said, with no sign of unseemly curiosity. "Are you sure it would not help to talk it over with a friend?"

"I'm sure it would," she admitted.

To her relief, the soup arrived just then to preserve her higher cerebral processes from alcoholic annihilation.

"Many problems that seem impossible alone become much easier if one talks about them," Jaeger observed in the most fatherly of tones.

"But this is such a *special* problem!"

"All problems are special to the person who has them. But I am a special kind of friend."

"But I hardly know you at all," Vicky blurted. Then she lowered her spoon and earnestly added, "Not that I mean anything by that. It's just . . ."

Curt Jaeger raised a reassuring hand.

"Don't apologize. What you say is quite true. On the other hand, the fact that we aren't old friends is my greatest advantage. I've often thought, in fact, that a stranger is the best friend one can have, assuming that he—or she—is particularly *simpático*. Because you can believe a stranger to be anything you like. For a little while, at least, a stranger can be one's ideal." He tapped a cigarette from a pack and added ironically, "Which probably explains love-at-first-sight—and the fact that one falls very easily in love with people one doesn't really know, but has a devil of a time becoming, or staying, infatuated with people who've been around for quite a while."

"You're right," said Vicky, impressed with the exposition but a little confused about what he was driving at.

"So, in brief," her companion said, "it's just because you don't know me that you can consult me about anything as impersonally as a doctor or a confessor. My disapproval— which I guarantee you won't have to face—couldn't bother you, but you could be sure that my advice would be quite impartial."

A waiter topped up their wineglasses while another took away the soup bowls.

"I'm not trying to pry, of course. If you want to tell me anything, put it in general terms, and I won't possibly be able to guess what you are referring to."

Vicky settled back against her cushion.

"Well, suppose you had a clue that might lead you to a fortune, like a buried treasure, but you didn't really have a right to it. I mean, it didn't really belong to you or anybody at the moment, but the only people who *would* have a legal right would be some government or other. What would you do?"

"You mean like these cases of sunken ships, where divers do all the work and then the government that controls the coastline steps in and scrapes off most of the profits? I assure you I would help myself to the treasure and let the government worry about its own welfare. They would certainly hear nothing from me."

Vicky smiled and raised her moisture-beaded glass to her lips with both hands.

"Well, that's a straight answer," she said. "I think I can probably swing my conscience around to that point of view."

"Yes," Jaeger concurred. "What could be less worthy of your guilty conscience than a government?"

"Especially when I don't even know which government," said Vicky, feeling more lighthearted than she had since leaving Iowa. "You're right. Why turn over anything to a bunch of stuffed-shirt bureaucrats?"

"Bravo!" Jaeger applauded. "And naturally you couldn't show your stewardess friend the mysterious letter telling about the pirate's gold, because then she would have been able to use the map to find her way there before you."

"She might, I suppose," Vicky said. "But . . ."

Suddenly Jaeger seemed struck by a disturbing thought that fitted aptly into her hesitation.

"I'm just thinking," he said. "Your friend, with all respect, probably has the same weaknesses as the rest of us, and her disappearance *was* rather abrupt. You don't suppose she could somehow have taken the letter—or perhaps be planning to take it while you're out?"

"Oh, no, Freda wouldn't have thought of such a thing! And even if she had, it wouldn't do her any good to try to find the letter."

"You hid it well?" Jaeger asked. "Or better still, put it in the hotel vault for safe-keeping?"

"Even better than that," Vicky said proudly. "I cut out the paragraph with all the important things in it—with all the directions—and memorized it, and burned it!"

Curt Jaeger's admiration was so very far from boundless that only the longest swig of champagne could quench the fire of rage and disappointment that rose unbidden into his face.

"That was really brilliant of you," he commented, with grim honesty hardening his smile. "I'm glad I am not some kind of foreign agent trying to pick your brain."

4

For Simon Templar, entering Vicky Kinian's hotel room was about as difficult an operation as sliding a hot spoon into a dollop of ice cream. But only paranormal powers of observation or intuition could have warned him that the girl whose private correspondence he intended to investigate was already being orbited by such a galaxy of variegated snoopers that it would have been impossible to approach within visiting range of her or her lodgings without entering the purview of at least one of them.

From the moment when he left his own room and crossed the corridor, he was, in fact, under the surveillance of the white-whiskered bald man who made such practical use of the aids to his infirmities: the cane was already fitted with its periscope extension, and the oversized hearing-amplifier was already switched on when the door to Vicky Kinian's dark room swung quietly inward. It had been partially by luck that the plump eavesdropper had detected Simon's movement across the passage; but now, with his gadgets

fully activated, he set about systematically following the
Saint's explorations.

Once in Vicky Kinian's room Simon turned on the lights,
glanced at the general layout, and began his search as coolly
as if he were paying the bill for room 302 himself. First, the
obvious empty suitcases, underneath the underclothes in
the chest-of-drawers . . . Success already amongst the lacy
silks. His hand brought forth an envelope slightly yellowed
with age. There was a typed directive on the front which
read: *For Victoria Kinian, on her 25th birthday, c/o William
F. Grey, Attorney-at-Law.* Inside was a cryptic note telling
daughter Vicky to visit Portugal and pick up a box at an antique shop in Lisbon. Hardly what could be called a cliff-
hanging letter. Almost certainly Vicky Kinian had already
gone there in the morning and come back to the Tagus
Hotel with something much more informative.

Simon kept on looking. Underneath the mattress of the
bed there was nothing but a chewing-gum wrapper. His
attention turned then to the massive mahogany wardrobe
which seemed to loom over the rest of the room as if it
considered itself immeasurably superior. Such old-fashioned
examples of the cabinetmaker's art, with double doors sur-
mounted by a carved cornice, had flat recessed tops ideally
designed for concealing dust, dead flies, and highly personal correspondence.

The Saint drew up a chair, stood on it, and looked down
on to the upper surface of the armoire. There his search
ended. Another envelope, larger and much fatter than the
first one, lay waiting for his attention. He took it, stepped
down, and pulled out the folded pages. There were nine in
all, closely written by hand, and sections had been cut out
of two of them.

Darling Vicky, he read. *What I am going to tell you can
make you a multimillionaire, but it may also lead you into*

great danger. Others will be after the same prize, and they aren't playing for fun . . .

Certain that he had found what he was looking for, Simon decided that there was no need to push his good fortune by lounging there while he waded through the whole long missive. Even if there was very little chance of Vicky Kinian herself returning so soon, a maid might come in to turn down the bed. He could continue reading in his own room. He moved towards the door and turned out the lights.

And behind him—without his ever having been aware of it—an angled combination of mirrors was quietly withdrawn from Vicky Kinian's balcony . . .

There had seemed to be no need to sneak furtively into the hotel's public corridor, and Simon stepped boldly out, intending to cross straight over to his own room. Then he quickly changed his plans, for coming down the hall towards him, and looking momentarily surprised when they saw him, were two of the most unsavory-looking beings ever to scuff the carpets of a respectable inn. One was small and scrawny, with moustaches like black stilettoes and a nose like the operational end of a poleaxe. His crony was bigger and more unwieldy, with overhanging brows and an underslung lower lip giving the middle portion of his countenance a positively recessive look, as if an impatient parent had once reprimanded him with a well-aimed billiard ball.

Neither of them said anything to the other as they approached, and Simon did not think that they recognized him, but at the same time he was sure that his appearance had startled them. They trooped on past him, looking dourly unconcerned, perhaps intent on some petty knavery which—so long as it did not involve him—the Saint did not have the time or inclination to worry himself about. But just in case they did have some special interest in him or in Vicky Kinian, he decided not to open his own door, which would have marked him as an obvious room-hopper, but instead to continue down the hall and downstairs into the lobby. If the two creeps he had just encountered had other business to attend to, they would assume that he had been just another guest leaving his own quarters.

He became aware even as he walked from the stairs into the lobby that he was being followed. Reflected in the glass door which led on to the street, he could see the same two worthies keeping what they must have considered a discreet distance behind him.

Simon went ahead out the door. He would walk around the block and see just how persistent his escort was.

Outside it was dark except for an occasional street light, and the sidewalks glinted with a sprinkling of rain just beginning to fall. There was thunder not far away out over the estuary, and a fresh breeze accompanied the summer shower. Sticking close beneath awnings and architectural outcroppings, the Saint could stroll casually without getting too wet. Then when he reached the corner the rain started to build towards its climax. He stood under a stone archway in deep shadow, watching the drops dance on the pavement. Half a block away, two other men, a small one and a bulkier one, stopped and waited in the shelter of a doorway. There was a five-minute pause, a silence relieved by rumbles of thunder and the occasional hiss of the tires of a passing car, and then the shower was over as abruptly as it had begun. Simon sauntered on his way, turning into a darker side street. In the strip of sky which showed overhead between rows of tiled eaves, the stars were already appearing between patches of scudding cloud.

Behind the Saint there was a distinct sound of footsteps.

"If those characters are just out for an innocent stroll, I'll give them a chance for a little more privacy," he mused.

He turned under an archway which led into a short alley which opened at its opposite end on to another dimly lit street. About halfway along the deserted arcade, he paused to listen.

After a few seconds' silence, a single pair of footsteps came quickly along behind him.

Without showing any visible indication, the Saint's body and mind went on combat alert. His muscles were relaxed and ready for swift movement in any direction, to meet any threat—including the rather clumsy threat that immediately became an actuality.

The man with the hypodermic-needle moustache and the Hallowe'en nose was holding the point of a knife in the immediate vicinity of his jugular vein.

"At once, *senhor!*" the little man ordered hoarsely. "Give me what you have in your pockets!"

The Saint, wishing to keep his blood to himself, thought it wise to eliminate the threat of the knife-tip before proceeding to deal with the comedian who was aiming it. He pretended to acquiesce, reached into one of his jacket pockets, and brought out the letter he had taken from the top of Vicky Kinian's wardrobe. With a sudden dramatic gesture he flung the white envelope aside into the shadows.

"Is that what you were after?" he asked mildly.

In the first instant that this enemy's attention was distracted, Simon struck like a snake. The rigid edge of one of his hands smashed the knife arm of the other man aside, and then with a twisting swinging combination of movements he flipped his opponent into the air, yanked him through a completely graceful somersault, and helped him to as ungentle a landing as possible flat on his face on the cobblestones.

As might have been predicted, the second attack wave lumbered on to the field as soon as the first had crunched to a temporary standstill. Arms flying, the bigger of the two strangers—obviously bringing into play all the subtle chivalric skills learned in a lifetime of a dockyard brawls—

hurled himself into the combat. Hoping to achieve an out-flanking triumph he lunged to whip a thick arm around the Saint's throat from behind. But the Saint caught the arm before its trap-like action was completed, brought the elbow joint against the fulcrum of his shoulder, and all in one magnificently flowing gesture levered his huge assailant up and over and dropped all two hundred pounds of him flat on the pavement not far from the site of his colleague's plunge.

The said colleague, in the meantime, was dazedly scrambling to his feet, clawing at the Saint's coat. The bigger thug gasping for breath, grabbed for Simon's ankle. The battle, though now distinctly onesided in favor of the outnumbered force, was far from over, and it swayed and thudded along the whole length of the dark arcade.

There was a fourth, unseen, participant in the episode, who then moved in to take advantage of the confusion for his own purposes. Only a single element in the drama interested him at all, and that was the white envelope which now lay abandoned in the deep shadows where the fight had begun. He waited his chance, then sidled swiftly along the stone wall, snatched the letter off the ground, and darted away again with an agility amazing in a man of his stout build.

He emerged into one of the side streets on which the alley opened, and the faint rays of a street lamp fell across the whiteness of his Vandyke beard. At the opposite end of the alley he could see the combatants silhouetted in an archway. One of them fell heavily and cried out, and in a moment of sudden alarm the plump man with the beard was afraid he had been seen. He turned and ran, and was still running when he rounded the corner leading on to the main street and ran almost directly into the unsuspecting arms of a pair of damp-shouldered policemen whose minds, until that moment, had been on nothing more violent than the latest international football match.

The bald and bearded runner, so obviously in full flight, knew that he had to come up with an instant explanation.

"*Policia!*" he cried breathlessly. "In there! Murder! Men fighting!"

His Portuguese left much to be desired so far as elegance of phrase was concerned, but the gist of his meaning was quite clear. The cops propped their caps more firmly into place and took off at a run, while the public-spirited civilian who had given the alarm was left behind shouting and pointing.

"In there! Someone is being killed!"

The policemen disappeared into the arched alley, and the bearded man, tucking the white envelope into an inside pocket, could not suppress a smile of unmitigated smugness. Then, like a busy fat crab, he scuttled away into the shadows.

The gendarmerie, meanwhile, had arrived on the scene of the crime with billy clubs waving, only to find a single tall unruffled man turning from two groaning hulks prostrated at his feet. Sizing up the situation instantly, they each grabbed one of the arms of the tall man and pulled him away from his victims.

"Villain!" keened one of the officers indignantly. "What are you doing assaulting these citizens?"

Simon was able to reply in faultlessly colloquial Portuguese.

"You've got it upside down, boys," he answer calmly. "I'm the one who was getting assaulted."

On the face of it his assertion was not obviously credible, and the guardians of public order can perhaps not be censured for escorting him into the light at the end of the alley and demanding to inspect his papers.

"You'll see from my passport that I'm a simple tourist,"

Simon assured them, with injured innocence. "Those thugs attacked me and tried to rob me. I'd suggest you grab hold of them instead of . . ."

He looked towards the men he had left polishing the cobblestones with their shirt fronts. They were struggling to their feet and setting a course which would take them as fast as possible from any opportunity to congratulate their uniformed rescuers.

The Saint pointed commandingly.

"As you'll notice," he said, "they aren't waiting like honest characters to register a complaint. Personally, I intend to report your behavior to my embassy."

The aristocratic appearance of their captive, as well as the evident justification of what he was saying, was enough to convince the policemen that they might very well be making a mistake of the sort that can have most embarrassing consequences. Without waiting to hear any elaboration of the details with which he would regale his embassy, they ordered him to wait where he was while they chased his attackers. He was only too glad to oblige, and as soon as the cops had taken off around the corner after their rapidly limping quarry he pulled out his fountain-pen flashlight and hurried to the spot where he had thrown Vicky Kinian's letter.

He expected to see the envelope immediately, and it took him only a few seconds to realize that it was nowhere in the section of the alley where he had thrown it. And yet there was no chance that one of his sparring partners could have grabbed it; he was certain that he had kept them too occupied during the whole *mêlée*.

Simon whirled quickly and sprinted after the two policemen. Now that the rainstorm had passed there was no wind to have blown the envelope away, and the only other obvious possibility was that one of the cops had noticed it and snatched it up on the run.

In the narrow street beyond the alley, down to the left, the sounds of the chase were still near, and took the form of sharp shouts and a confused skidding of feet, at least some of them flat.

"In there! He can't get out!"

"That way! The other one!"

As Simon raced on to the dimly lit scene it became clear that the two fugitives had split up, and that only one of them had had the foresight—or good luck—to pick a route which might conceivably lead to a prolongation of his malodorous career. The second one had made the error of getting himself cornered in a cul de sac full of garbage bins. The Saint arrived in time to see him—the little roach-like entity with the moustache—caught in the powerful beam of one of his pursuers' electric torches, struggling with the closed rear door of an apartment building which formed the end of the architectural trap. He was shielding his face with one hand and clutching his long knife in the other.

The policemen immediately showed signs of recognition, if not of joy.

"Halt, you unprintable unspeakable!" yelled one of them.

"Halt or I'll shoot!" shouted the other, snatching out an automatic, but still keeping a respectful distance.

The prodigal obviously anticipated that the Lisbon police force would stop depressingly short of barbequing a fatted calf in honor of his return to the land of the Godly, and in fact were more likely to barbeque him, and this no doubt caused him to panic. Instead of obeying the commands of his pursuers, he took the ungentlemanly and imprudent step of throwing his knife at them, hoping to make his getaway through the apartment building's back entrance before they could recover their balance.

But there are days in everybody's life when little things seem continually to go wrong, and it was such a day in the life of Pedro the Population-Adjuster. Little things like a wrong turning and a tightly locked door added up to a moment of acute inconvenience as a cop's finger squeezed a trigger twice and caused two notable perforations in Pedro's anatomy just above his hammered-silver belt buckle.

Pedro writhed to the ground and twitched to grotesquely sprawled stillness as the policemen strode to his side to pronounce their benediction.

"Misbegotten swine!"

"He should have had it long ago."

The Saint intervened.

"I hate to intrude on your sorrow, boys," he said, "but I wonder if either of you picked up a letter I dropped in the alley back there?"

The two officers became aware of his presence once again.

"*Senhor!*" one of them hailed him in congratulatory tones. "You were quite right. There is no blame on you. This pig is known to us, and we have finally caught him in one of his crimes!"

"To say the least," Simon concurred, looking down at the bloodsoaked body at their feet. "I wonder why he was after me?"

"Oh, *senhor*, he would do anything—stick you up in a back street, kidnap your children, kill! Anything it would pay him to do, he would do. He has been in jail four times —since he was a boy."

"Five times," the other officer corrected.

"No, it was four. The last time—"

"And probably it ought to have been forty-five," Simon cut in pacifically. "But now that he's no longer a problem, I'm more interested in my letter. Did you happen to find it as you passed through the alley?"

"Letter? No, *senhor*. No letter."

Both men shook their heads, confirming to each other that they had found nothing.

"But if you will come to the station with us, *senhor*, you can describe the other villain and answer questions that may produce . . ."

Simon declined politely and gave them a half-salute of farewell.

"I have already seen justice done," he said. "I am satisfied—and there is a lady waiting for me who will be most unsatisfied if I am much later in meeting her."

"But if you are wanted as a witness, *senhor?*"

He calmed them down by showing them a passport with a genuine photograph of himself on it and giving them the name of a hotel at which he was not staying. Having no complaint against him, and perhaps preferring to recite the epic of their deeds to their superiors without any burdensome touches of realism from a stranger, they let him go then, and as he walked away the last words that reached him were: "I will bet you a bottle of Ferreirinha that it was four times!"

Actually the Saint scarcely heard them. He was too preoccupied with the sudden new spine-tingling awareness that he was no longer a free-roving agent circling the perimeter of a situation and leisurely debating his own possible points of entry. Someone even farther outside and still beyond his ken was watching *him*.

III: How the Saint continued
the Pursuit, and was
Observed in his Turn.

"I hope you won't think I'm rude," Vicky Kinian said. "It sounds ridiculous to turn down an invitation to a night club on my first night in Portugal, but I'm absolutely bushed. I feel as if I hadn't slept in a week."

Curt Jaeger was as sympathetic as ever.

"I don't blame you," he said as he escorted her across the lobby of the Tagus. "And from the sound of what you told me at dinner you have an even more exhausting time ahead of you."

Vicky nodded and wearily started up the stairs.

"I'm getting worn out just arguing with my conscience about the whole thing."

"If I were you," Jaeger told her, "I would go on and find this treasure while I was arguing with my conscience. It might be an amusing adventure, and if in the end you decide not to keep it, you should at least be entitled to a finder's reward."

His reasoning appealed to Vicky, since it allowed her to

do what she wanted to do while telling herself that she was really not doing it.

"I'll think about it," she said when they had come to the door of her room. "Anyway, I'll be going on as soon as I can arrange it."

"Going on?" he asked.

"I might as well tell you, it's such a coincidence and you've been so nice. I have to go to Switzerland next. I can't see any harm in telling you that."

Jaeger almost laughed.

"You do lead a merry chase," he said. "But the fates seem to be conspiring to keep us together. Of course I too will be going to Switzerland, to my head office, when my business is finished here—which it almost is."

"Well, I'm glad the fates brought us together here," Vicky said. "The dinner and the champagne were delicious. And you were very kind to listen to my troubles."

"Not troubles—opportunities," he said. "And in case you should worry, let me assure you again that as a point of honour I am as anxious as you that no one else will ever learn what you have told me."

They shook hands then and said goodnight. Jaeger went back down the stairs to his own room, while Vicky, faint with tiredness, unlocked her door and pushed on the light switch just inside.

For an instant she thought that the strain of the past few days was making her see things, for lounging perfectly relaxed in an armchair half-facing the door was the tall devastatingly magnetic man she had noticed downstairs in the lobby that afternoon.

She froze, stared, and her next thought was that she had walked into the wrong room.

"I'm so sorry . . ." she began, but before she could even start to retreat she collected her wits enough to notice a pair of her own shoes on the floor near the bed, and her cosmetics on the dressing table.

By now the visitor had risen unhurriedly to his feet.

"You needn't be sorry," he said in a soothing tone. "Please come in."

Vicky's impulse was to turn back and call for help, but the man's manner and the almost supernatural holding-power of his blue eyes—as clear and bright as a tropical sea even in the yellowish illumination of the hotel room—kept her where she was, poised on the threshold.

"This is my room," she said unnecessarily. "What are you doing here?"

The man seemed to resist the temptation to make some lighthearted joke.

"I'll be glad to answer that question, Vicky, but it'll take a little while," he told her. "If you'll please come in and sit down I'll tell you. Right now you look like a doe ready to bolt for her life."

"I am ready to bolt," Vicky assured him. "You tell me what you want, and I've got plenty of wide open spaces behind me in case I don't like what I hear."

He shrugged.

"At least you're willing to listen," he said. "We're making progress."

"I think I'll get the manager," the girl said uncertainly.

The lean, towering man looked around innocently.

"If you need help, I'll be glad to oblige. What's the problem?"

She did not return his glimmer of a smile, but she was no longer quite so tensed for flight.

"All right," she said. "So you've given me a chance to scream or make a run for it, and if you'd wanted to hurt me you could have hidden somewhere and grabbed me after I closed the door. But that still doesn't mean we're old buddies. Who are you?"

"My name is Simon Templar, sometimes called the Saint, and I'm not dangerous if taken as directed. Why don't you shut the door and let me start convincing you that I'm on your side?"

She had reacted sharply to the sound of his name, and now she studied his face with heightened interest.

"The Saint?" she repeated incredulously. "Why should I believe that?"

"Would a passport convince you?"

She was already convinced enough to risk leaving the doorway and coming forward far enough to take the booklet he held out to her. Still keeping a safe distance, she looked at the photograph and the pages crowded with visa stamps. She half-smiled as she handed the passport back at full arm's length.

"So a celebrity broke into my room," she said whimsically. "That makes it all right, I guess. What did you do—pick the lock?"

"I was afraid it might compromise your reputation if I asked the room clerk to let me in. So I did what any gentleman cracksman would have done."

"Well, *that* certainly needs explaining, even if you are the Saint," she retorted indignantly.

"It was quite easy, really. I'll show you the trick if you're interested."

"I mean, *why* should you want to get into my room?"

He took a step towards the open door, and she moved back so that he could not cut off her escape route.

"Wouldn't it have been out of character if I hadn't?" he answered unassumingly. "I mean, think what a disappointment it would be if the Saint showed up politely ringing your doorbell with his hat in his hand."

"And that's the only reason?" she asked sarcastically.

"I'll be glad to discuss this if you'll close the door," he

replied. "Just in case there are any bog ears flapping down the hall."

"Mighty thoughtful of you," she conceded. "Okay, I'll take a chance—but if you do anything funny I'll scream my head off. You stay over there by the sofa and I'll stay over here."

Simon agreed with an amused shrug, and settled his rangy frame on the sofa cushions. Vicky Kinian shut the door, and perched uneasily on the arm of a chair not far from it.

"Now," she said, "please tell me what's going on."

"I will; but bear in mind that I agree in advance that I'm completely unscrupulous—so you can spare me any outbursts of righteous indignation." He crossed his long legs and swung one arm along the back of the sofa. "I broke in here the first time when you went out to dinner. I was looking for a certain letter . . ."

Her dark eyes flashed angrily, and she glanced towards the top of the wardrobe.

"Well, I never heard of such—"

"Gall," Simon supplied helpfully. "And if I hadn't found the letter at the time that reflex of yours would have given away where it was hidden."

She was on her feet.

"Well, you can just give it back to me right now!"

The Saint's face showed genuine regret.

"I would if I could, Vicky. Unfortunately you have more followers than Moses did when the going was easy—and I was set upon by a couple of rude fans who were ready to go to any extremes to get a souvenir."

"Who? Where?"

"A couple of unsavory types who were disfiguring the corridor when I came out—I would guess with ideas of combing out your room themselves. I tried to start a false scent by marching straight on out of the hotel, but they followed me up the street with the notion of finding out whether I'd brought anything valuable with me. I man-

aged to discourage them somewhat, but during the short
but merry tussle your letter still managed to disappear. I
searched all around while the cops chased my playmates,
and I checked with the cops after the chase was over, and
all I can deduce is that some other ardent admirer of yours
—some fourth party—picked it up and ran off with it while
the rest of us were getting our exercise at the other end of
the alley."

"Brilliant!" commented Vicky. "Now nobody has it!"

"Not nobody—just somebody unknown. Maybe you have
a clue as to who it might be—and it's certainly important
now for you to tell me what was in that letter."

The girl's temper was at the flash-point.

"Well, if that doesn't take the blue ribbon! You'd think
it was *your* letter or something. You haven't even started to
explain what you're up to!"

"All right," he said in a business-like voice, "I can't prove
to you—or even risk telling you in a room that may be
bugged—just how legitimately I found out why you're here
in Lisbon. But if you want proof in the morning I'll supply
it. In the meantime, I'll just say that I know in a general way
what you're after, and I know that there are some pretty
vicious parties on the same trail." He studied her keenly.
"It occurs to me that you may not even realize how much
danger you're in—and what kind of rough characters are
in this paper chase with you."

"Why, no, I didn't," she answered in honeyed tones.
"You're the first one I've met."

"Think it out for yourself," Simon urged her, unabashed.
"This other character has the letter now, anyway—and his
methods prove that he's up to no good."

"Of course, your methods are perfectly normal and prove
that anyone ought to trust you," she responded.

"As I said, I can't prove much of anything at this hour of
the night," he admitted patiently. "Maybe we should con-

centrate on the point that you now know that your father's secret isn't completely secret, and that the hounds of the Ungodly are even now sniffing at your threshold."

Vicky glanced fearfully towards the door of her room.

"At my threshold?" she breathed.

"Figuratively speaking. And when they come after *you* in some dark alley, you may be very glad to have somebody on your side who knows at least as much about these sorts of shenanigans as they do."

The girl's distracting mouth hardened.

"Shenanigans is right," she said brusquely. "And you, I suppose, are the knight in shining armour who's going to defend me through thick and thin."

"In two easy clichés, that's it," Simon said.

"Well, I'll tell *you* what's going on," she said belligerently. "You stole my letter, found out that the most important part was missing, and now you're giving me this nice saintly story to get me to tell you what was in it!"

Simon rose and faced her.

"I've told you the truth. I'd only just started to read the letter when—"

"A nice trick, but it's not going to work, Mr Templar," she interrupted. "I memorized the part that had the important instructions in it, and destroyed it so nobody else could find it—and it's going to stay that way!"

She had to admit to herself that the Saint looked genuinely concerned.

"But don't you see, if that's true you're in even more danger," he said urgently. "If the other side knows you did that, they'll go to any lengths to find out *from you* what was in it. Don't forget what happened to your father . . ."

"Nobody knows," she said, wanting to contradict him in any way she could.

"Exactly," said the Saint. "You, too, could disappear."

She was determined not to give in.

"And so could you—if you could take a fortune with you! I think I've heard a few things about the Saint's affinity for loot." She stalked to the door and threw it open. "And now will you kindly leave, or have I got to call for help? There's no reason on earth why you should be so anxious to save my skin. You're just trying to get your hands on something that doesn't belong to you."

"And that may not belong to you either," he pointed out.

"The difference is that I know more about it than you do, and you won't fool me into giving up that advantage."

Simon took a very deep breath, and finally walked past her into the hall. He turned again after he had assured himself that it was deserted and that no other doors seemed to be ajar.

"I can't say I don't admire your nerve," he said. "I just wonder if you've got the muscle to back it up. Well, if things start to look too tough, just let out a reasonably loud scream, and I'll try to be within range."

"I don't believe your story about some other gang being after the same thing at all," she returned defiantly. "I think you're just trying to scare me!"

She closed the door hurriedly, turned the key in the lock, and leaned against the varnished woodwork with one hand over her pounding heart as her lips added soundlessly:

"*. . . and you've done quite a job of it!*"

2

The Saint was awakened next morning by the ringing of the telephone beside his bed.

"Good morning!" said a booming baritone.

"Is it?" inquired the Saint, with reasonable curiosity.

"This is Jim Wade—Embassy. Just thought I'd check in and see how it's going."

Simon looked at his wristwatch and the almost horizontal rays of sunlight which slipped between the drawn curtains that covered the French windows.

"You boys must have a long working day," he remarked. "Do you always hit the desk by seven-thirty in the morning?"

"Not always, but I've got big brass breathing down my neck on this thing. Any luck yet?"

"No more than usual, but I had a couple of middle-aged delinquents with full-grown switch knives breathing down *my* neck in an alley last night."

"You mean there's somebody else in on this too?"

"In brief, Colonel, we are not alone. There are more bloodhounds on Vicky Kinian's trail than you could shake a steak at. I wouldn't be surprised to see TV cameras being set up down in the lobby for live coverage."

He quickly filled in the intelligence officer on the events of the night before.

"So you see," he concluded, "it's something of a standoff so far—but that was only the first round."

"These men who jumped you—could you figure anything else about them? I'll check with the local police, of course."

Simon, already sitting up in bed, punched a second pillow behind his back to make himself more comfortable.

"They were local talent, I'd say, from their looks and accent, but hoof-and-knife men only. They were obviously recruited by somebody who knew what to tell them to look for."

"And with the only one who was caught dead, nobody's likely to get much information out of him," the colonel reasoned unimpressively.

"I could make two guesses about their employer, and they could both be right," Simon said. "Obviously there were

Nazis who knew what Major Kinian was trying to find out
—and they, or some of them, may still be around."

"Besides which," Colonel Wade put in, "other intelligence
services than ours may have been on the same track that
Kinian was."

"Exactly. So we may still have both oppositions to cope
with today. And so could the gal. There's a character staying
here with the intriguing name of Curt Jaeger—Swiss passport—that she's already gotten friendly with, or who's gotten
friendly with her. Took her out last night. Of course, it could
be just a harmless pick-up, but you might try to find out
more about him."

"Curt Jaeger." Simon could visualize Wade jotting down
the name. "Okay . . . It would make our job a lot easier if
we had some idea of exactly what Kinian may have gotten
on to before he disappeared. Any ideas yet?"

"A few. While Miss Kinian was gently throwing me out
of her chambers, she let the word 'loot' slip out—and something about my wanting to get away with a fortune. Any
escape hatch a Nazi bigwig was counting on would've certainly had plenty of boodle stashed along the route."

Wade's voice was suddenly grimmer.

"You're thinking Major Kinian stumbled on a cache like
that and planned to pick it up for himself?"

"Or left a clue for the folks back home in case he sevened
out—which I have a strong feeling he did."

The colonel grunted thoughtfully.

"I hate to think one of our guys could've decided to take
a profit like that, but it's the most likely possibility. Weirder
things have happened. A lot weirder. Now . . . if this gal is
just an ordinary kid, she might respond to the 'good citizen'
approach. After all, she's led a perfectly respectable life
until now."

"It might work," Simon agreed, "but only you could make
that pitch. She might trust the uniform, and if you could

bring along a small flag to wave it wouldn't hurt either. I suggest you hurry, though. I have a feeling she's not going to waste any time."

"Don't worry," Wade said smugly. "She can't fly the coop without us knowing it. I've got a man watching the hotel. I'll give her a call now and shoot right on over there."

"Maybe you should just shoot over without calling first," the Saint advised. "She's pretty jumpy."

"Will do," replied the colonel smartly. "You sit tight, okay?"

"Okay, but don't let on to the girl that you know me, in case a good healthy streak of self-interest proves stronger than philanthropic patriotism. After all, the government dumps a few million down rat-holes every month, and she puts in eight-hour days for ninety dollars a week. I have a feeling you'll still be needing me after you try the friendly persuasion."

In order to stay out of the way while the officially certified forces of righteousness had their go at Vicky Kinian's conscience, Simon had breakfast sent to his room. He had scarcely finished the last bite of a juicy pear when his telephone rang again.

"This is Wade," said a defeated baritone. "She turned me down.

"No go, hm? Didn't take long."

"No. I got her to meet me in the lobby, and she just kept claiming she didn't have any idea what I was talking about." Wade coughed unhappily. "The only thing else was, she started complaining that the army and the government never did anything special for her father's dependents—and what was I doing turning up now trying to get something out of her?"

Simon chuckled.

"I'm beginning to think she's got the coldest shoulder this side of Point Barrow. What next?"

"I'm dumping it back in your lap, Saint. Like you said, she still thinks you're on your own, and maybe if she runs into real trouble she'll be only too glad to turn to you for a helping hand. In the meantime, we've got contacts at your hotel and the travel agencies. If she should be thinking of leaving town I think I'll hear about it pretty fast and I'll let you know."

"Good. You say you've got a man watching the hotel?"

"Right."

"Then why don't you have him keep an eye on her movements? They're nice movements, but she knows me now and she's liable to spot me if I stay too close for too long. I'll hang around in the background until we see what's up, and I'll phone the hotel desk occasionally in case you've left any messages for me."

The Saint shaved and dressed, and about half an hour later he went downstairs to the lobby. Leaving his own key at the desk, he observed that the key to room 302 was in its slot.

The same clerk to whom he had confessed his admiration of Vicky Kinian the day before was on duty again.

"Miss Kinian is already out?" Simon remarked disappointedly. "I don't suppose you have any idea where she went?"

He gave his question additional priority by extending an example of the national currency halfway across the counter between two fingers as he asked it.

"I gave her the name of a travel agency, *senhor*," answered the clerk, making the bill disappear on his own side of the desk with consummately unobtrusive prestidigitation. "She also asked my advice about sightseeing and I recommended a few places of interest."

"A travel agent?" Simon asked with unhappy surprise. "She is leaving, then?"

"She is leaving the hotel this afternoon, *senhor*. She wishes to fly to Switzerland. If you wished to begin a friendship with her, *senhor,* I am afraid you have not had enough time."

"Perhaps I shall have to follow her to Switzerland," Simon said jokingly. "You don't know which flight she's taking?"

The clerk shook his head and glanced at another customer who was waiting his turn.

"I am sorry I cannot tell you more. Perhaps at the agency just around the corner . . ."

"Fine." The Saint hesitated before leaving. "The sightseeing she mentioned—do you know . . ."

"She wanted to know how she could see the most places in a short time, and I suggested to her the bus which makes a tour of the city in three hours." The clerk glanced at his wristwatch. "It stops in front of the hotel here to take on passengers at eleven."

"Is it one of those tours that herds the sheep from church to church and gallery to gallery and allows them fifteen seconds to gawk at each masterpiece?"

The clerk smiled deferentially.

"I am afraid so, *senhor.*"

"I think Miss Kinian will be very occupied, then, and well taken care of without any help from me," Simon reflected aloud. "Maybe I shall have better luck later."

He had just thanked his informant and turned from the reception counter when the clerk called him back from the switchboard with which he also had to divide his attention.

"*Senhor!* Please, a call for you. Would you like to take it in your room or here?"

"In my room, I think. Have them hold the line for just a minute."

As Simon climbed the stairs he considered the relative advantages and disadvantages of joining Vicky Kinian on her sightseeing tour. It seemed probable that she was motivated by a real desire to see some of the sights of Lisbon before leaving. With only a few hours left before she flew to Switzerland, she would want to fill in the time as touris-

tically as she could. After all, she might be zeroing in on a
fortune, but while she was in the process she was just a
thrifty Iowa girl bedazzled by her first glimpse of Europe.
If she expected to pocket her bonanza in Lisbon, she wasn't
likely to choose to do it in the company of forty other
rubbernecks.

The Saint unlocked the door to his room, locked it again
behind him, and picked up his telephone.

"Hello, Mother," he said brightly.

"It's Wade again," replied a disconcerted, low-pitched
voice.

"Just thought I'd fool any wiretappers, but now you've
given the game away. What's up?"

"The girl, she's made reservations to—"

"Fly to Switzerland?" Simon suggested.

"How did you know?"

"A pal of mine decided to sing for his *vinho*. But I didn't
get the hour of departure."

"She's leaving on the Air Europe flight at four-thirty, for
Geneva. I just got a call from our contact at one of the travel
agencies. She seems to be travelling with that man you mentioned—Curt Jaeger. He bought a ticket on the same flight.
Know anything more about him?"

"I'm afraid not," Simon answered. "I'm counting on your
organization for that. In the meantime, our gal is booked
on a sightseeing bus tour which leaves here at eleven. Do
you think your watchdog on the spot could trail along?
She's liable to drop the whole idea if I show up and try to
hold her hand, but I'd like to feel that somebody was pro-
tecting her."

"Affirmative," said the colonel efficiently. "Will do. What's
your next move?"

"I'll try to catch a plane earlier in the day and pick up my
gorgeous little prey and her friend again at the Geneva air-

port. I'll give you a ring from there to be sure nothing catastrophic happened after I left."

"Sounds like the best program," Colonel Wade agreed. "If nothing else happens, I'll hear from you from Switzerland. I'm afraid you'll have to be on your own there until I can arrange . . ."

"I'd prefer it that way," Simon said. "Don't arrange anything. Just see that Vicky gets on her plane safely. I'll take care of the rest at the other end of the line."

3

The Saint landed at the Geneva airport at five-twenty in the afternoon—by which time Vicky Kinian would have taken off from Lisbon in another plane headed for the same destination. As soon as he had cleared Customs he found a telephone booth and rang up Colonel Wade back in Portugal.

"The girl left on schedule," the intelligence officer told him over the crackling line. "This Jaeger character was with her. From what my man could overhear on the sightseeing bus they're just friends—and not very close ones at that. Jaeger's a respectable businessman as far as we can find out up till now. Sales manager of some kind of Swiss watch export company, which explains why he's going to Geneva."

"But not why Vicky is," said the Saint. "I'll be waiting under the Welcome mat when they light here. You'll be hearing from me."

"Good luck, Saint!"

The first thing that impressed Simon when he emerged from finishing his business was the crisp freshness of the Swiss air as contrasted with the humid sea level atmosphere he had left behind. The second phenomenon that impressed

him was a stout, bald, rather scholarly looking man whose
facial topography was somewhat concealed between a Vandyke beard and a pair of steel-rimmed spectacles. He left
the telephone booth which shared a common wall with the
one Simon had used, and stayed in the same area of the
lobby. When the Saint paused to glance over the magazines
displayed at the newsstand, the white-bearded man took an
interest in a display of chocolates a few feet away. When
the Saint moved on to study the arrival-and-departure
boards, the stout man concerned himself with the purchase
of a newspaper.

Simon felt certain he had seen the man—without paying
any particular attention to him—on the same plane he had
taken from Lisbon. Why should he hang around the terminal building and, by chance or design, not let any great
expanse of waxed rubber tile get between him and the
Saint?

Simon deliberately walked off at a brisk pace towards
the far end of the lobby. The other man did not follow, although it was possible that his eyes tracked Simon's chang-
ing position from behind his thin-framed glasses. A short
while later, as the building became more crowded with
passengers and their friends, the bearded man turned,
tucked his paper under his arm, and strode out of one of
the doors towards the taxi stand as if whatever mysterious
business he had had in the lobby had suddenly been
consummated.

Simon relaxed more completely and tried to decide
whether the episode had really been an episode or whether
it had been no more than a suspicion in an alert and un-
charitable mind. If Grandpa Trotsky did not reappear, well
and good. If he ever materialized as an innocent lurker
again, it would be time to consider countermeasures.

There was a U-Drive car rental kiosk in the lobby not far
from where the Saint was standing when his bewhiskered

friend left the scene. Simon went over to it and spoke to the gray-uniformed brunette behind the counter.

"Salutations, Lieutenant," he said cheerily. "I wonder if you have anything in the motor pool that would suit me."

The girl touched her pert forage cap self-consciously and gave him a smile that seemed to say, "If you'd like to see me in something more glamorous, just ask . . ." But as is usual with girls in real life, what she actually said was less exciting.

"I'm certain we do, *m'sieur*. What kind of automobile would you need?"

"I'd like to hire something that's fairly fast but not too conspicuous. Bigger than a breadbox but smaller than those chrome-plated hearses you rent to couples from Miami."

"A Volkswagen, *m'sieur*, or . . ."

"A Volkswagen is fine."

The formalities took only a short while, and when he was putting his signature on the completed forms the counter girl asked him, "What hotel will you stay at here in Geneva?"

"I don't know yet. Where I go depends on some friends who'll be in a little later. As soon as I've settled on one I'll phone you."

"Can I do anything to help you?"

Simon regarded her.

"If I told you," he said regretfully, "I'm afraid you'd tell me that your Hertz belongs to Daddy."

When his friends did arrive, the Saint was waiting for them in his green Beetle near the terminal building's entrance. He watched as Vicky Kinian and a tall man came out of the swinging glass doors and waited to step into a taxi. The girl's companion—sharp-featured, with closely trimmed light hair—held the cab's door for her, gave an order to the driver, and got into the back seat himself. Simon did not recognize him; even from a number of yards away he could be sure that their paths had never crossed before. There was no way to tell yet, then, whether Herr Jaeger's

main interest was in attractive American girls or some more
negotiable and enduring embodiment of pleasure, perhaps
in the form of several tons of SS gold at the bottom of an
Alpine lake.

The taxi pulled away from the curb. Simon had already
started his car. Now he accelerated after the cab, not hesitating to stick quite close behind it during its trip into the
city.

While the Saint followed, Curt Jaeger was beginning to
doubt his once considerable powers as an interrogator. All
the way from the green-and-brown coats of Portugal to the
white icy crags of the Alps he had been subtly trying, without the slightest success, to lead Vicky Kinian on to the subject of her treasure hunt, and in particular on to the events
which he knew had taken place the night before.

He had waited in his room at the Tagus after coming
back from dinner with Vicky, expecting his telephone to
bestir him at any minute with a ring from Pedro reporting
on his search for her letter. A great many minutes had
passed—one hundred and forty-eight, by Jaeger's own count
—before the telephone did ring, and then the breathless
voice which blabbered ungrammatical Portuguese over the
wire did not belong to Pedro.

"This is Fano, the driver. I know where you at so I call.
Pedro, he's dead—shot by the cops!"

A moment of panic had threatened to shatter Jaeger's
usual self-control; but recalling the necessity for superior
races to maintain a firm facade when dealing with such low
forms of life as Portuguese cab drivers, he had managed to
keep his voice completely steady.

"Do they know about me?" he asked.

"They do not know nothing," replied the driver emphat-
ically. "I hear Pedro was dead the minute they plugged
him. So it's all right if you pay me."

"What did you find in the girl's room?" Jaeger asked without optimism. Vicky's revelation during dinner that she had memorized and destroyed the vital part of her father's letter had already made Pedro's search of her room seem hardly necessary.

"We didn't go in," was the answer. "A man come out—had a letter on him."

"Came out?" Jaeger asked impatiently, straining to understand the difficult accent. "Out of what?"

"This man, he come out of the girl's room. We followed him to an alley. Pedro took him and there was a big fight. Then the cops come and we run—"

"Without the letter?"

"We couldn't get it," the thug said excitedly. "Like I tell you, the cops come, shoot Pedro. I beat it out of there."

"This man who came out of her room—do you know him? Who was he?"

"Don't know. Very tall, black hair, eyes blue . . ."

"Thin? Fat?"

"More thin—like a matador. Strong as hell—and quick!"

The Latin began appealing to his gods and their female relatives to witness the inhuman power and swiftness of his foe in the alley fight. Jaeger interrupted him again.

"And you found out nothing else?"

"No, but we done as you told us, so you can pay me. You can pay me for Pedro too. I give to his widow."

Jaeger had needed all his powers of self-restraint to prevent himself from screeching hysterically.

"You are a stupid idiotic oaf," he had said coldly. "If I ever see you again or hear from you again, it will be your fortunate widow who needs a donation."

He had slammed down the receiver and spent many feverish hours during the wakeful night raking his brain for some clue as to who the stranger might be who was threatening to interrupt his long, long climb just before he reached the pinnacle.

In the taxi with Vicky in Geneva, he tried once more. Surely, he told himself for the hundredth time, if someone had broken into her room and taken something, she would be aware of it—and eventually admit it to him. He was, after all, her only friend in a foreign land.

"I am worried about you," he insisted. "Perhaps I can ask one question that will not seem like prying into your secrets . . ."

"Worried about me?" Vicky asked.

She had spent most of the flight, as well as the drive between airport and city center, in a pensive, quiet, apparently almost depressed mood.

"Yes. Is it possible that anybody else could be looking for the same thing as you may be?"

Vicky's reaction was not at all sophisticated. She glanced at him sharply.

"What made you ask that?"

"A simple logic," Jaeger said offhandedly, raising a cigarette to his lips. "There are few secrets of which rumors do not reach the wrong people. Luckily you need not worry about the little you have told me. I said I was a salesman of watches, but to be less modest, I am owner of the agencies which distribute them, and frankly I have too much money to be tempted by your story."

"I'm not very experienced about anything like this," Vicky began, but Jaeger went on.

"I only want to warn you to look out for some adventurer or other who may try to steal your secret or talk you out of it. If anything like that happens, would you tell me?"

Vicky stared at him for a few seconds before she answered.

"I think you're a mindreader, Curt. As a matter of fact something did happen." She looked out of the window rather than at him as she went on, but her entry into Geneva carried none of the glamorous charge that had excited her when she had first arrived in Portugal. She was too preoccupied with worry and indecision about what she was doing to experience any very happy sensations. "It happened last night, while you and I were out for·dinner. Somebody broke into my room."

Jaeger's eyes narrowed.

"I was afraid of just that sort of thing," he said gravely. "Did he—the burglar—did he take anything?"

"He took the letter my father wrote me, and—"

Jaeger allowed himself to become agitated.

"Well, did you not report this? Did the police—"

"I have to tell you the rest," Vicky said evenly. "In the first place, you'll remember that I'd already cut out the part that mattered from the letter. But the most fantastic thing is, the man who took it came back to see me!"

This time Jaeger did not need to squander any theatrical talents on looking astonished.

"To *see* you? And you never said a word?"

"He was waiting in my room when you took me home," she explained. "And he had the nerve to offer to help me."

"Well, naturally!" Jaeger exploded. "He stole your letter, confirmed that you were after something valuable, and since you had cut out the important part of the letter he had to come back and find out more."

"Don't worry. I didn't tell him anything."

"Don't worry?" Jaeger exclaimed incredulously. "You're lucky to be alive! And you let this criminal go?"

"He wasn't a criminal," Vicky retorted with a sudden heat that surprised even her. "In fact, he almost convinced me . . ."

"You sound as if you're defending him," said Jaeger. "Who was he? Or I should say, who did he claim to be?"

"I probably shouldn't tell anybody—just in case I have to change my mind about him. If I'm going to be an adventuress I'll have to learn to think like one."

Jaeger almost glowed visibly with elder-brotherly exasperation.

"How could there be any doubt? If the man had had good intentions of any kind he would scarcely have broken into your room!" He turned in his seat to plead with her earnestly. "Vicky, have I not been a good friend to you? A new one, but one who has not given you the slightest reason to distrust his motives?"

"That's true," she said.

"Then you must—you absolutely *must* tell me who this man is! I know officials here in Geneva who can investigate him. It is utterly foolish for you to expose yourself to this kind of risk, and I won't stand by and allow it."

She looked at him with a new kind of fear in her eyes—one related to her own unconventional intentions.

"I don't want any officials poking their noses into my business," she said.

"All right," Jaeger replied more calmly. "They won't—if you'll tell me who this man was."

Vicky thought for a moment and then gave a defeated sigh.

"His name was Simon Templar—the Saint . . ."

4

Although the Saint's formidable reputation was strongly in the minds of both Vicky Kinian and Curt Jaeger when their taxi stopped in front of the Portal Hotel, they would probably have experienced something like the supremely invigorating shock of a bucket of ice water on the nape of the neck if they had been aware of his actual physical proximity. Mercifully for their adrenal equilibrium, they were not subjected to this brusque exhilaration; although when they walked into the hotel, Simon was watching from his car only a hundred feet away, and when Curt Jaeger came out alone a few minutes later the Saint was able to take a long unobstructed look at his face before he got into another cab and rode away.

Simon was less impressed by Vicky Kinian's sharp-featured boyfriend than he was by the hotel she had chosen. Apparently the prospect of future riches had completely subverted her ingrained standards, for from a one-horse elevatorless hostelry in an unpretentious quarter of Lisbon she had seen fit to remove herself to one of the finest examples of solid understated elegance in Geneva. The Portal was directly on the lake, and beyond the braid-draped doorman who stood beneath its crested marquee the Saint could watch the course of sails and speedboats across the calm water.

He did not watch for long, however. Once Curt Jaeger had been carried well out of sight by his taxi, and once Vicky Kinian had had ample time to get herself and her luggage to her room, Simon himself let the doorman usher him into the quiet bronze and gold of the lobby. Within three minutes he had signed for a room and seen his bags carried away to it. Without bothering to inspect his new lodgings more thoroughly, he used a lobby telephone to notify the car-hire agency of his whereabouts, and then went back to the Volkswagen he had rented from them, unfolded a newspaper, and prepared to wait as long as necessary for Vicky Kinian to make her next move. He could only hope that whatever she had to do next involved an actual excursion of some kind on her part, and not some such less detectable form of communication as a phone call. He was also gambling on the probability that she would be too anxious to get on with her quest to sit around the hotel for the remaining few hours of summer daylight.

While Simon waited, and while Vicky unpacked and

changed her clothes, a new member of the Kinian caravan
was going into underhanded action back at the Geneva airport. The Saint had, in fact, seen him not many minutes
before, but he had been no more than a rather ugly face
among a great many other unimpressive faces in the terminal building. The only thing which might in any way have
made him memorable was his nearness to the bald man
with the white Vandyke whiskers just before that dawdling
character had made his abrupt departure from the airport;
but there had been a host of other people in the same area
too, and it would have taken a full-time paranoid to suspect
them all.

The new character's name, for the convenience of our
own record, was Mischa Ruspine, and his dour countenance
seemed to be suspended limply between two protrusive
ears which resembled a pair of not quite identical outsized
teacup handles. Sheltering that wholesome and inviting
physiognomy was a display of unwashed brown hair that
started thin on top, gathered momentum behind his ears,
and ended in a thick climactic heap on his coat collar. He
was indeed an associate of the persistent eavesdropper in
the white Vandyke, and just before that latter party had
forsaken the airport terminal he had muttered out of the
corner of his mouth:

"The tall man with black hair down by the photograph
machine."

"Hm," Mischa had confirmed identification.

He had received his instructions earlier, so no further
dialogue was necessary. He watched his assignment stroll
to the booth of a car rental agency, and managed to stand
inconspicuously near enough to overhear most of his conversation with the uniformed counter girl. What he heard
convinced him that he could combine pleasure with business by relaxing in the terminal bar and returning to the
U-Drive agency later. There was no point in wasting energy

and running the risk of losing the Saint in traffic as he followed him, when he could instead wait in comfort and then follow with perfect certainty about where he was going.

So Mischa had sipped his way through two cold lagers, stretching them over thirty minutes, and then had shuffled back to the car rental booth. His normal gait was somehow as dour as his countenance.

"I have something to deliver to a Mr Templar," he told the girl. "He said you would know what hotel he had gone to."

The girl looked at him with ingenuous surprise.

"Your timing is very good," she said. "He just telephoned. He is staying at the Hotel Portal."

"*Merci, mademoiselle.*"

"Do you know where that is?"

"*Oui, mademoiselle.* I do."

His next stop was at a telephone kiosk near the terminal exit. He dialled a local number and within a few moments heard the voice of the man in the white Vandyke.

"*Realité Foto.*"

"This is Mischa. I have the information. He hired a car at the airport to drive himself, and then followed the other two when they left."

His revelation failed to spark enthusiasm at the other end of the line.

"I could have predicted that without leaving you there to watch. But where did they *go?*"

"Templar has registered at the Portal," Mischa answered. "Obviously the girl stays there too."

"Are you sure he did not see you following?"

"I was too smart to follow. He said he would let the car renters know which hotel he chose, so I waited until he phoned them."

In spite of Mischa's smug self-satisfaction, the reaction of his superior was still anything but congratulatory.

"Then you can be still smarter and go there prepared to
begin following—and at once! What if Templar has already
left the hotel? You may never pick him up again. And the
girl . . ."

"Do not worry," said Mischa. "I am on my way."

"The thought that you are on your way is most unlikely
to relieve my worry. Hurry, and report back when you have
something worthwhile to tell me!"

The phone connection clicked abruptly dead, and Mischa
turned sulkily from the kiosk and ambled with deliberate
slowness out to the airport's public parking area, then pan-
icked at the thought of possible failure in his assignment
and exceeded the speed limit all the way to the Hotel
Portal. There, to his immense relief, he saw Simon Templar
sitting by the curb in his rented Volkswagen reading a newspaper.

Smugness returned. Mischa parked his car at a safe distance behind the Saint's and began his own share of what he
correctly assumed to be the wait for Vicky Kinian.

It was almost half an hour later when she came out of
the hotel and had the doorman call her a taxi. The Saint's
car spat smoke for an instant as its engine caught. Mischa
turned the key in his own ignition. The procession set off
along some of the less-travelled streets of Geneva, away
from the central city.

Mischa, who knew the town well, speculated with each
new turn about their ultimate destination. Even so, he was
completely surprised when the rear lights of the Saint's car
flashed red as he approached the entrance gate of the International Cemetery. The cab carrying Vicky Kinian pulled
over to the curb. The Volkswagen's brake-lights went off
and it whipped on past. For an instant Mischa was undecided, but his orders gave priority to following Simon Templar. As he zipped past the taxi, Vicky Kinian was getting

out and walking towards a flower vendor beside the cemetery gate.

The Saint's car moved on beyond the graveyard, made
a U-turn, and stopped just out of sight of the entrance gate.
Mischa's car flew past, made a U-turn, and stopped just out
of sight of the Volkswagen's occupant.

The cemetery was set in a locale which permitted such
automotive acrobatics to take place without much danger
either of smashups or police intervention. The road was almost unused, and the countryside immediately around the
graveyard's perimeter was a preserve of rocky slopes and
evergreens which might have been fifty miles into the Alps
instead of on the outskirts of a bustling city.

The cemetery itself was an uncrowded community of
quiet stone whose streets were deserted pebbled walks and
whose houses were marble sepulchres. Scattered yew trees
and ranks of solemn monuments cast long shadows across
the grass in the red light of the sinking sun. Following on
foot behind the Saint, Mischa could see Vicky Kinian walking uneasily among those shadows, a spray of white flowers
clutched like a protective talisman in one of her hands.

She seemed unsure of her course, but after each hesitation she would start out with an air of fresh confidence, as
if she had satisfied herself that she was heading in the right
direction. It was easy for Mischa to saunter, hands clasped
behind him, in the distant background, appearing to admire the herbaceous borders which lined the footpaths. It
was obviously less easy for the Saint to make himself inconspicuous, since he, unlike Mischa, was known to the
girl. He kept well away from her, using trees and the massive walls of mausoleums as cover for his apparently innocent movements.

Suddenly the girl stopped and then walked forward rapidly until she came to a very large monument set back in a
semicircle of shrubs and trees. Mischa, from his faraway

vantage point, could not make out the letters carved into
the stone above Vicky Kinian's head, but he could tell that
the monument was no ordinary one. It was like a semicircu-
lar wall of granite ten feet high and twenty feet or so wide,
topped by a great stone eagle with wide drooping wings.
The concave front of the structure was faced with a bronze-
framed glass door behind which there seemed to be several
shelves.

Mischa could observe nothing more from where he had
to wait his turn for a closer view. Vicky Kinian stood close
against the glass door and studied whatever lay behind it
for almost twenty minutes. Several times she looked around
to make sure nobody was watching her, and she seemed to
be having trouble making some sort of decision. Finally she
hastily stooped and dropped her bouquet on to the semi-
circular stone step that formed a low platform in front of
the monument. Then she turned and walked away through
the cemetery at a much faster pace than she had used when
she had come in.

The Saint did not follow her, so Mischa waited, now moving closer to the big monument, concealing himself behind
a conventional tombstone more notable for lavishness of
proportion than good taste. Simon Templar, once the girl
was completely out of sight, went and stood in front of the
glass-fronted memorial himself. In less than two minutes he
turned away and strode back toward the cemetery's gate.

Now Mischa could have his own turn at the Cimetière
Internationale's suddenly most popular landmark. He hurried up to the curved granite structure, gazed dolefully at
the doleful face of the carved eagle, and read the lettering
which the bird protected with outspread wings.

HIER RUHTE DIE ASCHE DER FREIEN DEUTSCHER
DENEN ES DAS SCHICKSAL VERWEHRTE, IN IHR
VATERLAND ZURÜCKZUKEHREN.

The words translated themselves automatically in Micha's mind: *Here rest the ashes of free Germans to whom fate denied a return to their Fatherland.*

Behind the glass door, which was locked flush against the granite, were four shelves, each bearing a row of ten small metal caskets.

Mischa had no time for meditation on the meaning of it all. He turned again, and by walking fast managed to bring the Saint within his purview near the cemetery gate. There followed another tripartite procession back to the Hotel Portal, where Vicky Kinian and Simon Templar got out of their respective vehicles and went separately into the lobby. Mischa walked to the bar across the street from the Portal and telephoned his supervisor, his voice betraying unmitigated self-approbation.

"I have interesting news," he said.

"Useful as well as interesting, I hope," snarled the man at the other end of the line. "Has he been anywhere? Have you lost him?"

"Of course I haven't lost him!" Mischa said indignantly. "He has just come back to the hotel, and I can see the entrance from where I am. He seemed to tell the doorman that he would be inside only a few minutes."

"You are a mindreader as well as a hunting dog. Tell me everything Templar did while he was out."

Mischa described his processional tour of the graveyard.

"This gravestone that they were both looking at," his bearded superior said with great interest. "Tell me more about it."

"That is all I know. It was a monument to Germans who died in Switzerland during the war. It is full of ashes."

"And of what else? Something much more intriguing than ashes, I have no doubt. The girl or Templar will go back for whatever is hidden there as soon as they think it is safe. But you must see that they do not get it."

"I shall take tools and go as soon as it is dark," Mischa said.

"Go now!" the other man responded impatiently. "What if somebody should get there before you?"

"I go," said Mischa with dignity. "But what about the Saint? I cannot watch him also."

"You concern yourself with whatever is in that shrine," was the reply. "I shall occupy myself with Mr Templar!"

IV: How Curt Jaeger failed to
    Levitate, and Mischa's Efforts
    were Rewarded.

All the intensely individual interests which had been launched like homing missiles in the general direction of Vicky Kinian from such diverse silos as Washington, Tokyo, and the American Midwest, and Simon Templar could only speculate where else, had now converged upon a single city, and even two small parts of that city: a place of accommodation for the living and a place of accommodation for the dead, the Hotel Portal and the Cimetière Internationale. And some of the personages involved in Vicky Kinian's treasure hunt were soon to find that the shortest route between the two locations was not necessarily a straight line.

The Saint, returning to the hotel from the cemetery after observing Vicky's fascination with a memorial to German exiles, had not for a moment forgotten the mysterious disappearance in a Lisbon alley of a vital letter that he had not had time to read, and was continuously alert to the uncomfortable fact that he himself might be under somebody else's watchful eye. But unless he had searched behind each potted plant in the Portal's lobby like the folkloric old spinster looking under beds, he would have had no way of knowing that Curt Jaeger, ensconced in a low chair behind the additional cover of the largest newspaper he could buy, was watching every step he took towards the elevator with an ardour that should have wilted the foliage of his verdurous ambuscade.

The Saint had one objective in his own mind at the moment, and although it had some concern with the dead it was considerably less violent than the thoughts that were reaching their logical climax in Jaeger's head at just the same time. Jaeger was a man of quick decision who believed in the tactical value of a minimum of delay and a maximum of force. He had done his homework. He knew what Simon Templar looked like and he knew his room number. Now it was only a matter of putting a simple but utterly deadly plan into effect.

When the elevator doors had closed behind the Saint, Jaeger got up from his chair, put aside his newspaper neatly folded on a nearby table, pressed one arm close against his ribs to feel the reassuring hardness of the thing that was concealed there, and followed the path his prey had taken across the Portal's thick carpet.

The Saint, in the meantime, had reached his room on the sixth floor and was taking from a drawer a small wooden box which opened into an inexpensive (so that it would not arouse the evaluating instincts of Customs inspectors) traveller's chess board. When the chessmen were put aside, only a twist of the box's catch was necessary to reveal the false bottom where—in a bed of cotton—lay certain implements designed to circumvent the locksmith's most cunning defences. The mechanism that held the door of the German memorial tombstone closed was a good one, but there was sure to be something in the Saint's kit that would quickly overcome its resistance.

He did not know what he would find in that macabre oversized strongbox, but he admired the ingenuity of whoever had chosen it as an open-air bank vault and he was determined to get to it ahead of Vicky Kinian. She would spend some time pondering how to break into it, and in any case she would almost certainly wait until it was dark before she took any action. While she was being cannily cautious, the Saint would exercise qualities more natural to him and open the shrine while there was still a little daylight left.

He glanced out of the window of his room as he slipped the chess box into his jacket pocket. The sun had already disappeared and the street lights down in the street six floors below were beginning to win their competition with the fading glow in the sky above. Simon felt sure that if he hurried he could be back from the burying ground in time to invite Vicky Kinian out for a truce dinner and a pipe of peace before she even began to get up her nerve to leave the hotel.

There was, however, a slight preliminary delay.

Simon turned from the window, strode to the door of his room, and opened it to find himself looking straight at the open snout of a large black automatic. Just beyond the automatic, and balanced like a man who knew and was ready for the recoil of a large-calibre pistol, was Curt Jaeger.

"Step back and let me in," he commanded in a low voice, "or I'll shoot you on the spot."

He was already on the threshold, and the Saint had no encouragement to doubt that his visitor would carry out the threat with the least reasonable provocation. Simon moved backward into his room as the other man, just slightly shorter than himself, stepped inside and closed and locked the door behind without taking the concentration of either his gun or his cold eyes off the Saint's face.

"Why, you must be Curt Jaeger!" Simon said cordially. "I was wondering when you'd be dropping in to swap a few war stories."

"So you know who I am," Jaeger said, not allowing himself to betray any great surprise. "That will save tiresome questions."

The Saint had stopped near the middle of the room. Jaeger, keeping a cautious distance, held the automatic aimed steadily at his chest.

"Not entirely," Simon said. "You must have been on this treasure hunt for a long time, if your dossier reads anything like I think it does. I just haven't figured why the big shots of the Third Reich would've shared their biggest secret with a punk bully-boy like you must have been in 1945."

"They did not," Jaeger replied. "All who knew the details died in Berlin or Nuremberg. I happened to be in Portugal at the end, and . . . But why should I be telling you anything?"

"Because you must be bursting to regale somebody with tales of your exploits after all these years—and because I think you'd love to rub my nose in your colossal brilliance before you rub me out. Unless of course you just dropped in to get my autograph or tell me to be out of town by sunrise."

Jaeger's slight nod indicated his appreciation of the Saint's logic.

"I happened to be in Portugal and to catch up with your Major Kinian, who had killed one of our top agents and taken information from him that was known—until then— only at the highest levels. I was lucky enough to catch Kinian and be the only one to question him—and I have waited too long to use what I learned to let you rob me!"

The Saint was completely relaxed, his hands loose at his sides.

"Apparently you aren't such a genius at asking questions if you waited this long and still haven't found the goodies."

"Kinian was wounded already, and I had to use rather heavy methods to get his cooperation. Unfortunately he died before he could finish talking, but he said enough to tell me that I only had to wait until his daughter was twenty-one, and watch her."

"Only now you don't have the exclusive on that," said Simon.

"In a moment I shall," Jaeger retorted with grim quietness. "Step back and open the window."

"It seems cool enough in here to me already," said the Saint. "In fact the atmosphere is downright chilly."

"Your comfort is the last thing that interests me at the moment. Do as I tell you. Step backward to the window and open it."

Simon still stood his ground.

"It's getting dark in here, and while I don't want to cast any aspersions on your marksmanship I'd hate you to mess me up with a lousy shot. The light switch is right beside you."

The harsh line of Jaeger's lips warped into the trace of a smile.

"Thank you for your kind advice, but I have no intention of giving a shooting exhibition on a floodlit stage. Just open the window."

The Saint stepped slowly back to the tall window, which reached from knee level almost to the ceiling. Before he reached for the handle which would swing it open he spoke to Jaeger again. He felt sure that nothing he could say would have any effect on the other's murderous intentions, but as long as he could stall them there was at least a chance that his luck might produce some kind of accident or interruption that would throw Jaeger off guard.

"If you're really determined to pop off that little cannon, wouldn't you rather have the window shut so it'll make less noise outside? I could even draw the curtains."

"Your thoughtfulness touches me deeply," said Jaeger. "But you must take me for an idiot."

"A natural mistake," Simon said apologetically. "All I really had to judge by was your face."

Any hint of amusement which might have been on Jaeger's lips had completely evaporated, and his voice was hard and biting.

"I am not here to waste time talking. Open it!"

The Saint opened it. As the glass swung outward, a breeze sharp with the feel and taste of Alpine ice swept into the room, rustling the heavy drapes. Even in summer the peaks which towered not far from the city let nobody forget their snowy domination. Death and the white glaciers high above clouds in the moonlight seemed brothers at this moment, and the Saint sensed that the dark wind which swept down from them had coursed through his whole life, filling every instant with the crystalline tingle of supernal frost.

The barrel of the black pistol was levelled at his chest.

"Turn around," Jaeger said softly.

"Maybe we can make a deal," the Saint said without moving. "Has it occurred to you that I might have some information you could use?"

"No, it has not," Jaeger answered, "and I don't believe that anything you say could convince me. I've done well enough so far on my own, and I don't need any deals with anybody. Turn around and face the window."

"If you shoot," Simon said calmly, "there'll be people all over you before you can get out of the door."

Jaeger's voice crackled with a tension like static electricity.

"Turn around immediately!"

The Saint obeyed, shifting his position so that he stood facing the open window. Ahead of him, across a wide void of empty air, was the tall apartment building that faced the Hotel Portal from the far side of a traffic circle. Below, just beyond the window ledge but a long way beneath it, were the canopy of the hotel's marquee, the taxis with headlights like flashlight beams, and foreshortened views of miniature people.

Behind him, Simon could hear Curt Jaeger moving, stepping very quietly across the carpet towards the window. A sensation of warming confidence began to spread through the Saint's veins.

"You wouldn't be thinking of saving ammunition, would you, Curt?" he inquired. "Considering something even sneakier than a shot in the back—and less noisy?"

Jaeger, predictably, made no reply, and just as predictably he came on towards Simon's back. The Saint's acute hearing measured each step the other man took, plotted his distance, noted the rustle of the material of his jacket as he raised his gun arm above Simon's head, poising the heavy barrel before smashing it down on the back of his skull.

Then, with a timing that allowed only the shaving of a second's error, the Saint exploded into action. His whole body ducked and whirled just as Jaeger chopped down with the automatic, and it was only Jaeger's wrist that landed on Simon's shoulder—a harmless blunting of the blow that was to have cracked his head with a handful of steel.

In the same tornado of movement that saved him from being knocked out of the window, Simon turned from defence to offence. One of his elbows smashed into Jaeger's ribs and sent him staggering away. With a speed and balance that left his adversary in total confusion, he continued his pivot, snatched Jaeger's gun arm, and with a bone-shattering chop of his straightened right hand bashed the pistol out of the man's fingers to the floor.

Jaeger gave a yelp of pain and struck out wildly with his other fist. It caught Simon harmlessly on a protective fore-arm, but his own fist was more effective. It made forceful contact with Jaeger's anatomy in the vicinity of his private beer-cellar, doubling him up and flinging him back against the wall not far from the open window.

"Give up, chum," Simon said. "You didn't figure on having to fight for your loot, and you've gone too soft to handle anything tougher than a lightweight female."

Jaeger, wheezing for breath, grabbed up a sharp-edged glass ashtray and hurled it at the Saint. It flew past Simon's ear and thumped on to the sofa.

"If you mistreat the crockery I'll have to ask you to leave," said the Saint.

He went after his opponent again, and Jaeger countered by trying for a clinch, tangling Simon's arms with his own and using all his weight to push him back towards the window. The Saint balked, braced himself, and freed a hand. He cocked back his fist and unleashed a short jab at Jaeger's nose. Jaeger staggered, letting go his grip on Simon, and launched a vicious kick.

The Saint caught the flying foot in midair.

"Sorry to behave badly for a host," he said, "but I'll have to ask you to leave."

With both hands on Jaeger's ankle he whipped him around in a perfectly timed swing that sent the other man not against the wall this time, but straight at the open window . . .

And suddenly there was only one man left in the room.

Simon braced himself on the window frame and looked down, secure in the knowledge that there were no lights on to reveal his interest to anybody in the street below or in the neighbouring buildings. There was a hole in the glass outcrop of the marquee six storeys down, and great excitement among the people on the sidewalk. Jaeger's sudden ungainly appearance in front of the hotel was already public knowledge, but nobody—unless someone had happened to be looking directly upwards as he made his unsuccessful attempt to defy the force which controlled Newton's apple —would know from which window he had fallen.

The Saint felt no remorse. Jaeger had taken precisely what he had intended to dish out, no more and no less, and nothing could have been fairer than that.

Simon checked to make sure that his double purpose chess box was still in his jacket pocket, and went to the door—a means of egress he much preferred to the one the late Curt Jaeger had planned for him. He would be out of the hotel before the police could begin to unfurl their clumsy nets, and Curt Jaeger's Luger—the only thing which could connect the Saint's room with the fallen man—would go with him.

2

"*Ghoul*," Vicky Kinian said accusingly to herself.

"An apéritif, *mademoiselle?*" the white-haired waiter asked.

Vicky looked up from the spotless surface of her small table. Outside the sidewalk café of the Beau Rivage the Quai du Mont-Blanc was almost dark. Within half an hour she could safely proceed with the task ahead of her. In the meantime, she wondered, what would be the best booster for a girl who was about to do her first job of grave-robbing?

"An Old Fashioned," she said, and then remembered she was in Switzerland and not in the Kit Kat Steak House in southern Des Moines. "Oh, I don't guess you'd have that . . ."

"Of course, *mademoiselle*. Immediately."

The aged cupbearer limped away to fetch her drink, and Vicky continued to meditate nervously on her immediate future. She told herself that she was not really a grave-robber, of course, since her father's instructions clearly specified which of the urns in the cemetery shrine contained not human ashes but something—just what she still did not know—much less necromantic and much more valuable. All she had to do was break through the monument's glass door and take the metal box marked JOSEF MEIER, and then run —no, walk—out of the graveyard. It was not really so ghoulish, and it would all be over in a matter of minutes.

The old waiter came back with her Old Fashioned. She bypassed the vegetation and gulped down the whisky, gratefully feeling the warmth hit her stomach all at once and begin to filter through her bloodstream.

She looked out at the street again. Passing cars were using their lights and she could no longer think of any excuse to delay. She fumbled too much money on to the table and left the café without waiting for the waiter to express his appreciation. Within a few seconds she was able to hail a passing taxi. She had vaguely hoped that every means of public transport in Geneva might by some fortuitous circumstance be occupied or out of working order for the next twelve hours, thus depriving her of the opportunity of doing what she both longed to do and dreaded.

But the cab driver, against all the laws of cab drivers' temperament, did not even twitch a querulous eyebrow when she asked him to take her to the Cimetière Internationale, much less turn her down flat as she was secretly hoping he would. He phlegmatically pushed his meter and his engine into gear, and took off towards the desired location with distressing speed by the most efficient possible route.

All Vicky's hopes for blowouts or mechanical disasters came to naught, and within an incredibly short time she was being ferried along the almost unpopulated road on the edge of the city which led to the entrance of the cemetery.

"Cimetière Internationale?" the driver called over his shoulder, as if giving her a last chance to change her mind.

"Yes," she answered.

A few minutes later the automobile came to a stop in front of the open gates which she had passed through earlier in the day. The area had no artificial lights, and the only illumination came from an almost full moon rising above the steep hills to the east. The many-shaped monuments in the graveyard beyond its barred fence looked like grotesque emerging creatures from an infernal world frozen in position for a moment by the sound of the car.

Again she almost changed her mind. She could simply sit where she was and tell the driver to take her back to the easy safety of the Hotel Portal. But that would also be going back to the easy dull safety of eight hours a day at the telephone office—and admitting that when her one big chance had come to make her life something more than a digit in the bottomless arithmetic of the Welfare State she had flubbed because she had the heebie-jeebies.

She got out of the taxi. She wanted desperately to ask the driver to wait, but she had already decided that that would be too risky. He could not see the shrine to German exiles from where he was parked, but the sound of breaking glass might easily carry to his ears through the quiet night, and in any case he could be a possible source of all sorts of complications. Besides he was pretending not to understand English as she questioned him about the fare, though he had understood her perfectly well when he had picked her up, which probably meant that he would have refused to comprehend that she wanted him to wait, even if she had asked him.

He took her money and drove away after giving her a final look which she was sure could only be described as pitying. She watched the red taillights disappear and then turned to face the cemetery gate. There was no sign of another living human being in any direction. On the road which circled the boundary of the graveyard there was not even the sound of an automobile to replace the frightening emptiness in her brain left by the departed taxi. Her only company was the lopsided ball of the moon which silvered the jumble of tombstones ahead of her.

Much as she disliked being alone in such a place, for strictly practical reasons she was far more worried about running into human than into ghostly interference. She thought she could safely assume that the Swiss, like most other people, had no taste for strolling in cemeteries at night.

Vicky took a deep breath and walked through the gate. She continued decisively and quickly down the gravel path towards the location of the German memorial. Something cautioned her, however, to avoid making too much noise, and as she got closer to the monument she slowed her pace and moved so quietly that she could scarcely hear her own footsteps.

Then she stopped.

She was almost within sight of the monument, and she thought that a faint scratching or scraping noise had come from its direction. Poised without breathing, she listened. The only sounds now were the background chirping and semi-musical sawing of nocturnal insects. It wouldn't have been surprising if her imagination had tended to embellish nature a bit.

She walked on, however, more cautiously than ever.

Turning a corner in the path she came within sight of the memorial silhouetted against the brilliantly moonlit sky. Its face was in deep shadow, but as she moved on towards it, approaching to within fifty yards, she saw a shadow stir. Something like true petrifaction seized her, so that she could not move even a finger. The dim shape by the monument moved again, but she could only make out that it was big enough to be human and was not a stray dog or cat.

Self-preservation almost screamed at her, urging her to run, calling in nightmare panic to set her feet moving. But Vicky Kinian had come a long way from her last schoolgirl Hallowe'en, and once having straddled life and gotten the reins in her hands she felt an even stronger instinct to hold on and not be thrown.

Suddenly anger began to replace fright. Somebody was meddling with *her* shrine, and she was not about to leave before she had at least seen who it was and what he was doing. She suspected that Simon Templar, true to his mystical nickname, had somehow found out the secret of the monument and was busily in the process of trying to steal her inheritance. If so, she would have no hesitation about walking up and bashing him on the head with her purse.

Her very readiness to attack the Saint in a lonely grave-yard with nothing more deadly than a handbag showed a certain faith in his gallantry which she did not recognize in herself until later. But that trust did make her careless. She did not take quite the extremes of care in sneaking up for a closer look at the memorial that she might have otherwise. She tiptoed from tombstone to tombstone, working her way towards the great stone eagle that brooded on top of the exile's monument, trying to make out what the figure at the base of the edifice was doing.

When she was within fifty feet she could make out the man's back. The scraping noise she had heard had apparently been the sound of a glasscutter. Now, using some kind of suction device with a short handle, he was removing the whole curved sheet of glass from the memorial's door and setting it on the ground beside him. She noticed that he did not then reach immediately for one of the metal boxes on the shelves inside, but stood there as if undecided what to do next.

Vicky decided to move nearer, and as she did the toe of her high-heeled shoe caught on a stone ridge surrounding one of the burial plots, and she almost fell. A pebble clattered. The man at the monument pivoted, stared about into the darkness, and slunk quickly away among the tombstones and scattered trees to her right.

She waited, surprised that the poacher had given up so quickly, and disturbed by a new realization: she had seen enough to know that the man beside the monument had not been the Saint. Who he was she had no idea. Nothing about him had been familiar, and though she had not seen his face as more than a shadowy blur she was sure she did not know him. Had he followed her earlier in the day, or did he have some other source of information? Crouched in the shadow of a gravestone, she turned over the possibilities in her mind while she wavered between running away as fast as she could, and waiting, as still as a terrified rabbit, until she felt the danger had passed.

The way of the rabbit seemed safer. The man had, after all, not seen her, and he might decide that the rattling stone signalled no danger to him. In that case he would come back soon and begin his work again. If he had been really frightened, though, he might leave the cemetery and give her a chance at the urns. Either way, there was no point in revealing her presence.

She waited a long time. The moon rose a short but quite perceptible distance further above the big memorial's stone eagle than it had been when she had first stooped and hidden in the shadows. There was still no sound or other trace of her rival's whereabouts. She decided finally, after many minutes, and when one of her legs had gone completely to sleep, that the man had done just what he had seemed to be doing: hurried away from the monument and fled as inconspicuously as possible out of the cemetery.

The thought that he had been so easily discomfited gave Vicky a new sense of her own powers. She stood up, got some circulation restored to her numbed leg, and walked with as much confidence as she could summon to the opened shrine. A musty smell came from the shelves, which were having their first exposure to fresh air for twenty-five years or more. Her eyes were becoming more and more accustomed to the darkness, and the moon was distributing more light as it rose higher, but even so she could just barely make out the name-plates on the metal funerary boxes. Luckily the position of the reputed remains of Josef Meier at the left end of the upper shelf had remained fixed in her mind since that afternoon.

Gingerly she raised her arms and touched the box with just the tips of her fingers. Finding herself still undemolished by divinely hurled thunderbolts, she took the full weight of the box in her hands and carried it into the moonlight. There was no lock holding the lid closed, only a sliding catch made of chrome, but the catch was hard to move after so many years and for several seconds she exerted all her strength in an effort to budge it.

She was so intently occupied that she did not hear the very slight rustling in the shrubs just behind her; or if she did, it remained in the periphery of her consciousness, automatically interpreted as the brushing of a wind-gust through the leaves. When the rustle suddenly became the crashing plunge of a heavy body through foliage not ten feet away from her, she was too shocked and horrified even to scream.

She whirled, and leaping at her was a shadowed figure

whose face—limp-featured and grotesque like a rubber mask—was as grey as death itself in the moonlight.

Stumbling back, she would have screamed then, but the man's hands were on her. Fingers clamped across her windpipe and closed off her nose and mouth. No trace of oxygen could get to her lungs and no cry could escape from her throat.

The man dodged behind her, pulling her back against him as he kept up his relentless deadly pressure. The small resting-place of Josef Meier fell to the ground. All she wanted now was air, but there was none for her in the whole universe.

As her sight dimmed, the moon, emotionless and cold, having seen many such things in its time, seemed to fill her whole brain like a painfully gigantic glowing bubble ready to burst.

3

The Saint walked inconspicuously out of the Hotel Portal, past a preoccupied desk clerk, and then past the swarm of excited gawkers who surrounded the broken body of Curt Jaeger which lay on the sidewalk just a few paces beyond the entrance doors. A lack of curiosity would have seemed particularly noteworthy under the circumstances, so Simon dutifully paid a last homage to his would-be murderer by momentarily craning his neck on the edge of the crowd in a mock effort to see the crumpled remains.

Then he hurried on to his rented car with as much urgency as he dared to show, and a few minutes later was speeding towards the Cimetière Internationale. He had intended to be there long before this. Now the sky was completely dark, and as he moved from traffic light to traffic light away from the center of the city he could catch glimpses of the not quite full moon above the tops of houses and between apartment blocks. If he had wasted too much time in his last waltz with Jaeger he might very well find that Vicky Kinian—or some less deserving party, such as a lieutenant of Jaeger's—might already have scooped whatever riches lay in the multiple tomb of the German exiles.

He could not afford to stop his car too near the cemetery gate. He cut its lights and coasted to a stop as near the entrance as he dared. Running the rest of the way to the memorial would have been the most efficient but not the safest course. He could risk a sprint only as far as the gate. Then, avoiding the noisy gravel paths in favor of the damp grass, he walked unerringly through the dark maze of tombstones towards the German shrine.

When he came within sight of it he saw something that brought him to an abrupt halt. Bent low in the darkness, he could make out the form of a woman on the ground and a man getting to his feet from beside her. The man was turning his attention to something else on the ground nearby, and the Saint, as stealthily silent as a Mohican, raced forward across the uneven turf.

A few yards behind the man he stopped, and then moved forward more slowly. When he was within striking distance, he cupped his hands to his mouth and gave a shout that might conceivably have caused some alarm even six feet below the graveyard's surface.

"Boo!"

The object of his salutation gave an unrehearsed standing high jump that would have won the admiration of an Olympic coach. Simon made no move to attack. He stood with his hands on his hips as his victim scrambled for new footing that would let him see and face the threat that had suddenly appeared out of nowhere. The metal box the man had been holding when he was surprised had clattered to the ground. Now he was fumbling a weighted leather bludgeon out of his pocket as he stared around frantically for a way of escape. But the Saint, tall and confident in the darkness, had him with his back to the center of the concave memorial.

"Come now," Simon said, "don't you believe in ghosts? You can't hurt me with that little bean-bag or anything else."

His opponent was apparently the skeptical type. He squared off, raising his leather cosh threateningly.

"You'll give yourself a heart attack if you don't calm down," the Saint cautioned. "Why don't you put that thing away and tell me a few true ghost stories—such as how a zombie like you managed to get out of his crypt before Hallowe'en."

In reply, the bludgeon lashed out, hissing in the air as its owner swung it at Simon's head. The Saint, with an almost imperceptible leaning back and to one side, avoided the blow and let it whistle harmlessly past his chin.

"I warned you about ghosts," he said.

The other man had thrown all his weight into the swing, and it was ridiculously easy for Simon to reach out, help his opponent to continue the motion beyond its intended limit, and hurl him off balance across an outstretched leg. The forced pirouette came to an abrupt and ungraceful conclusion when Simon's flat stiffened hand chopped down like a guillotine on the back of his enemy's neck and sent him sprawling unconscious on the paved path.

In the vacuum of silence that followed, Simon strode to the woman on the ground, knowing before he knelt and turned her face to the moonlight that it would be Vicky Kinian. His only immediate worry was whether she would be alive or not. With an eye out for any other night owls who might decide to crash the party, he turned the girl on to her back and reached for her wrist.

At first he could not find her pulse, and she was horribly white in the moonlight. Then, as he took a tentative new searching grip on her limp wrist she heaved a deep sigh and exhaled with the moan of a child having a bad dream.

"I guess you'll live," Simon murmured. "Though I can't say you really deserve to."

She could not have heard him, and he saw no need to rush her into consciousness. He lowered her head gently to the ground again and moved back to the man he had laid to temporary rest a short while before. Inside his jacket pocket was a Soviet passport, which Simon examined by the cupped light of a pencil flashlight.

"Mischa Ruspine," the Saint read, and failed to fit either the name or the face into his private rogues gallery. "Mischa Ruspine of euphonious name, how do you fit into this Bald Mountain lawn-fête?"

Mischa, instead of answering, gave every indication of having sacked out for the night. Simon left him to go to the metal box that the other had flung to the ground in his moment of sudden terror. It had landed upside down and open. When the Saint lifted it, a single thin packet wrapped in oilcloth fell to the cement. There was nothing else in the container—not even a dust-particle of the chemical constituents of one Josef Meier whom the box's name-plate advertised as resting therein.

Before the Saint could unfold the oilcloth, however, there were new signs of life from Vicky Kinian. She took several quick breaths, gave a little cry, and tried to sit up. Then she saw Simon's face clearly in the moonlight.

"You!"

"Well, good evening," he said soothingly. "Don't look so scared. I'm not the guy who mugged you."

She answered groggily.

"I . . . guess you weren't. I saw him . . ." She suddenly was frightened. "Is he—"

"He's still with us," Simon told her, "but he's had a visit from the Sandman and is now relaxing in relative peace. His name is Mischa Ruspine. Do you know him?"

With a helping arm from the Saint, Vicky sat up, propping herself with one hand.

"No," she said. "Who is he?"

"I haven't the faintest idea, except that he hails from Moscow. You're lucky to be alive, you know, playing around in dark places with characters like him. You must be more lucky than clever."

As dazed as she was, she managed to put some fire into her voice.

"And you're the most aggravating man I've ever had butting into my business. I'd be a lot luckier if I'd never seen you!"

"Oh, I wouldn't say that," Simon returned calmly. "If I hadn't surprised Mischa while he was glomming on to this, you might have been short one clue in your treasure hunt. Or is this the *summum bonum* we've all been cracking heads to get at?"

He held up the thin package that had fallen from the metal box.

"You give me that!" cried the girl.

Simon held it out of her reach, and when she tried to get to her feet dizziness overcame her and he had to help her back to the ground again.

"Easy, now," he said. "Wait till you're a bit stronger before you start getting rambunctious."

"You'll steal it," she mumbled.

"So will you if I let you," said Simon. "We can discuss ethics in a better place than this, though. Take a few deep breaths and let's get out of here, as they say at least once in every television show."

While she recovered from her vertigo he reached for the metal box which had held the oilcloth packet and made sure there was nothing else in it, nor any markings in its interior. Then he closed the lid and put the little casket reverently back in its place on the shrine's upper shelf.

"Alas, poor Josef! I never knew him well, and I suspect he was strictly an imaginary refugee. It would've been no problem to get permission to add another urn to the collection here."

"What is it?" Vicky asked anxiously. "What's in the package?"

"Something very light," Simon informed her carelessly. "And knowing your father, probably something absolutely useless, like an envelope full of coded nursery rhymes giving complete instructions for finding the Matterhorn."

"I don't think that's funny."

"I do," Simon said unblushingly. "Let's see just what dear old dad really is up to next—back at the hotel. I'd like to get moving before Mischa wakes up or somebody else comes along."

He helped her to her feet and supported her at his side as they walked slowly back to the cemetery gate and his car.

Behind them, glasses glinting in the pale light of the moon, a short rotund figure stepped cautiously from a group of trees, and a plump hand switched off the electrical current of a kind of hearing device.

The man with the Vandyke beard walked from his hiding place to the monument to German refugees. Out at the cemetery's boundary he heard a car engine start and move away through four gears. He could move and talk freely now. He went over to Mischa Ruspine and prodded him with the toe of a well-polished shoe. Mischa grunted and lay still. The man with the white beard kicked him in the waist several times with increasing impatience.

Finally Mischa revived sufficiently to realize where he was and to remember what had happened. When he saw the formidable broad figure of his superior standing over him he at once began to make excuses.

"It was not my fault, Comrade Uzdanov! I had the box and he took me from behind."

"He was not behind you when he hit you," Comrade Uzdanov corrected him. "I saw it!"

Mischa was kneeling, holding his bowed head in both hands. Uzdanov moved slightly behind him.

"I will make up for it as soon as I can find him again," Mischa said.

"There will be no need for that," Uzdanov said kindly.

His words veiled the fact that he was very quietly twisting the crooked handle of his walking stick and pulling it from the main section of the cane. If Mischa had not been so busy trying to still the throbbing in his head he might have looked around and seen the short slender shaft of steel which projected from the detached handle, glinting frostily in the pallid light.

Uzdanov placed a reassuring hand on Mischa's shoulder from behind.

"There will be no need," he repeated. "You are now only a man who knows too much, Mischa—and I cannot trust one with such a record of failures. So goodbye!"

On the last word he plunged the sharp steel spike deeply between Mischa's shoulders. A moment later he withdrew the stiletto from his co-worker's body and left him lying where he slumped. Then, on second thought, he turned and wiped the blade clean on the tail of Mischa's jacket before replacing it in the cane and locking the sections solidly back into place.

All things neatly attended to, Uzdanov turned on his heel and walked rapidly out of the cemetery whose population he had just increased by one. He was ready to stop listening and watching now. The time had come for action.

4

"I don't know whether to thank you or call you a rat," Vicky Kinian said sulkily.

She was huddled in the front passenger seat of the Saint's rented Volkswagen pouting like a disobedient little girl being whisked home by her father from the school principal's office. During most of the drive from the Cimetière Internationale she had kept quiet, nursing her hurt pride and throbbing head. As they came to the light-fringed boulevards that bordered Lac Léman she finally gave her vocal facilities a real test and found they were still in fair working order despite the ungentle massage Mischa Ruspine had given her larynx in the graveyard.

"I think you're horrible for following me and poking into my business," she opined. "Even though I suppose you might've saved my life."

"I suppose the deed was worth just about that much adulation," Simon replied cheerfully. "After all, there are lots of American girl tourists in the world; one certainly wouldn't be missed. Maybe I should just take you back to the cemetery."

Vicky sat up as if a loose spring had penetrated her seat cushion.

"No!"

"Then try to show a little proper reverence for your mental superiors. Remember, I warned you back in Lisbon that you'd find the going rough on your own."

"Don't rub it in," she answered resentfully.

"I won't, but I'm afraid the shocks are starting to come thick and fast now. Do you think you can take another one?"

She stared at him, alarmed at his tone of voice.

"Why? Has something else happened?"

"Yes, and you'll hear about it when you get back to the hotel anyway. It's about your pal, Curt Jaeger."

"What about him? And he's not my pal. I met him on the plane from New York purely by chance."

Simon concentrated with unusual intensity on making a left turn at an intersection.

"He's not anybody's pal now, because purely by chance he tried to throw me out of a window about an hour ago—and fell out himself."

Vicky gazed at him unbelievingly.

"You mean he's injured?"

"Quite fatally," said the Saint, with a perceptible lack of mourning. "Which is just how he wanted me because I was sowing a few weeds in the primrose path he was leading you down."

Vicky covered her face with her hands and started sobbing.

"You killed him!" she wailed.

"Gravity killed him, with the help of a large section of concrete pavement." He glanced at her. "I didn't know you cared so much about him, though."

She lowered her hands from tear-glazed cheeks and her next words were almost a scream.

"I don't! I'm having hysterics!"

"You're much too sophisticated now for hysterics," Simon intoned soothingly.

"I'm not sophisticated! I wish I'd never left Iowa!" Then she tried hard to get control of herself. "Well, tell me! Why would Curt Jaeger want to kill anybody? He's just a watch salesman."

"He's more a watcher than a salesman," said the Saint. "I told you that there were probably other competitors in this gold rush."

"But when he got on the plane in New York he couldn't possibly have known what I was going to do over here."

"He'd been keeping an eye on you for years, ever since the end of the war. He was one of Hitler's Gestapo buckos, and he was the one who was on the same trail your father was. When they met, I'm afraid your father got the worst of it."

"You mean that's what happened to my father? Curt Jaeger did something . . ."

Her words trailed off, and Simon nodded.

"I'm afraid Jaeger killed him. But before he did he found out enough about your father's plans to make him take a long-term interest in your whereabouts."

Vicky sat limply beside him, staring straight ahead.

"I feel numb," she said finally.

"And I don't blame you."

He was pulling the car into a parking space not far from the Hotel Portal. Vicky thought a minute longer and turned to him.

"Then you won't blame me for not trusting anybody, including you," she said. "I won't necessarily believe you, but why did *you* start following me?"

"I'm sure you won't believe me, but it wasn't with any idea of loot. I knew nothing about it at the start, and I've still got no real idea of what you're after." He shut off the Volkswagen's engine and killed the lights. "Somebody in Washington asked me to get in on the fun when the Pentagon heard you were taking a short-notice Grand Tour of your dad's old stomping grounds. Apparently some tax-supported computer has also had you in its memory bank for a long, long time."

"Then you were tied in with that army man from the embassy in Lisbon who talked to me?"

"Yes. It was through his good offices that I almost did a swan dive from six flights up on to Lake Geneva's moonlit shore. I did a few odd jobs for the cloak-and-dagger divisions during the Nazi war and they figured I knew my way around some old alleys better than most. As far as I can tell, they were merely assisting me to try on the old school noose again."

"You don't mean they *wanted* to see you get in trouble?"

"No. They just didn't care. I walk through the fiery furnace, and if I come out with my skin uncrisped Colonel Wade gets another oak-leaf cluster on his good conduct ribbon." Simon tapped the oilcloth packet inside his coat. "Which makes me hope very sincerely that more material rewards of virtue are wrapped in this little bundle from the beyond that your father has led us to."

"I'm glad you said *us*," Vicky put in. "When are you going to give those papers or whatever they are back to me?"

Simon shrugged and opened his door.

"I must quibble about the word 'back'. After all, when did you ever have them?"

When he had helped her out of the car on her side she immediately jerked her hand out of his.

"So you're planning to steal them from me?" she asked bitterly.

"Before we start using emotional words like 'steal', let's get our ethics straight. We not only don't know what we've got here, but we also have no idea who it belonged to in the first place. When we've settled all that we'll worry about who's stealing from whom."

He took her arm, tucked it around his, and walked with her to the entrance of the Portal, purposely keeping himself between her and the dark stain on the sidewalk which was all that remained of Curt Jaeger in that immediate vicinity.

"Meanwhile," he said, "now that you've heard everything I can tell you, why not come clean with the rest of your own story?"

"You know most of it already," she answered. "My father's

letter didn't tell me what I'd be looking for, and I don't even know if that package you've confiscated is the end of the line or not."

They passed across the hotel's lobby to the reception desk, where Simon asked for his own and Vicky's keys.

"You're staying here too?" she asked. "I didn't even think to wonder . . ."

"I thought it'd be cozier that way," Simon said. "It wouldn't surprise me at all to find out that half the guests in this joint belong to the Vicky Kinian Fan Club and Snooping Society."

He started them towards the elevators; but just before they reached the closed doors their way was partially blocked by a grave-looking middle-aged man in a neat business suit.

"I beg your pardon," he said in slightly accented English. "You are Monsieur Simon Templar?"

"Almost always," the Saint replied.

The stranger held out an identity card and studied Simon's face with a chess master's intense grey eyes for any reaction. Simon read the card without obliging him with the slightest twitch of a muscle.

"Ah, yes, Inspector Edval," he said coolly. "And what are you inspecting this evening?"

"What is it?" Vicky asked, her face a picture of worried confusion.

"This gentleman is a police inspector," the Saint explained. "He has probably been so kind as to come over to report on his progress in finding our wandering mynah bird."

Inspector Edval regarded him impassively before continuing.

"Do you know anyone named Curt Jaeger?" he asked.

"I never heard of him," said Simon positively.

He had shifted his position slightly so that he could ob-

serve Vicky without obviously looking at her. Her cheeks
had reddened. Her lips parted as if she was about to speak,
and then she lowered her gaze to the floor.

"This man, Jaeger, fell to his death from a window in this
hotel which could have been yours," Inspector Edval said,
with a precision which implied that his sentence had been
rehearsed several times before its début. "Have you any
knowledge of *any* man who might have fallen from your
room?"

"No," Simon said. "Since I've been at the Portal I've never
noticed anybody passing outside my window in any direction."

"You possibly were not here when the event occurred. I
have already questioned the hotel guests who were in their
rooms, just afterwards, but naturally when I saw one of the
names of the Saint on the register . . ."

He shrugged, showing that he felt there was no necessity
for further explanation. The Saint agreed with an understanding nod.

"I'm sorry I can't oblige you," he said, "but I haven't murdered anybody for days."

The inspector seemed not entirely satisfied with the answer.

"Just for the sake of thoroughness, would you allow me
to visit your room?" he asked.

"A sociable thought," said the Saint agreeably. "It would
seem downright caddish of me to refuse."

He gestured towards the nearby elevators, and his two
companions preceded him to the now open doors. A few
moments later they stepped out and walked a short distance down a corridor to room 614. Simon tried to catch
Vicky's eye, if for no other reason than to try to judge her
emotional temperature and the likelihood of her bursting
into choruses of confession at the first real pressure from

Inspector Edval. But Vicky kept her thoughts to herself and her eyes on the wine-coloured carpet.

"Here we are, Inspector," said Simon, hospitably swinging open his door. "I'm not quite sure what sort of traces a man leaves behind when he jumps out of a window, but you're welcome to try to find them if it'll relieve your mind."

Edval nodded and grunted his thanks. He first stood in the doorway and peered around the chambers from that vantage point like a respectably attired fox checking out a water hole before risking a direct approach. Simon observed, before closing the door, that a uniformed policeman had happened along the hall at just that moment and decided to pause in his promenade a few yards away. He gave the gendarme a jaunty wave before closing him out and turning back to the inspector.

"Good hunting?" he asked, with benevolent interest.

Edval began to nod repetitively at some agreeable thought of his own, and to shuffle towards the high window at the opposite side of the room. It was a wide window, and the only one in Simon's quarters. It was, of course, the one through which Curt Jaeger had made his spectacular exit from this vale of tears—the one through which he had so kindly aspired to help the Saint make a similar escape.

The window was closed now. Inspector Edval noted the fact with an intense interest possible only to an investigator who is still undecided whether he is on the right track or not.

"Your Mr Jaeger must be a real magician if he went out by this window," Simon remarked. "He closed and latched it behind him."

The inspector scrutinized the window at close range and then opened it.

"But it would not have been a great magic trick for anyone who might have thrown him out," he said stolidly.

He did not look accusingly at Simon as he spoke. He was leaning cautiously out, staring down through space along the approximate trajectory that Curt Jaeger's body could have described through the air.

"Why would anybody have wanted to throw him out?" the Saint inquired, with a sidewise look at Vicky, who still refused to notice him. "Was he selling forged football tickets or something?"

Inspector Edval stepped back from the window and faced him.

"He may have been selling watches, according to his credentials," he said humourlessly. "But I am now having a quick check on his identification made." He took a deep breath, like a man bolstering his lungs before an unpleasant task. "In the meantime, I must look around this room for signs of a struggle—and I must also ask if I may search you for any signs of having been in a fight. You would have no objection to such a search, I hope?"

For the first time since they had met the inspector, Vicky looked up from the vicinity of her toes and darted a calculative glance at the Saint.

"That's rather an odd request," Simon said. "It sounds almost like an accusation."

"I intend no offence," Edval said politely. "But neither the concierge nor the doorman are quite sure whether you went out before or after Jaeger fell."

Now it was Vicky Kinian's turn to take a deep breath—a breath such as the Sphinx might have taken just before breaking its immemorial silence.

"I think I can help you with that, Inspector," she said.

V: How Vicky's Inheritance was
Revealed, and Boris Uzdanov
identified Himself.

The Saint could stop a man's fist with comparative ease, but the problem of stopping a woman's tongue was another matter, beside which the raising of the Tower of Babel to stratospheric levels would have seemed a casual recreation.

His face, however, betrayed none of the unhappy thoughts which flashfired through his brain when Vicky announced to Inspector Edval her intention of making a statement. He looked at her with the mild resignation of a disinterested teacher to some weakwitted pupil.

Then someone knocked at the door.

"Party-crashers," Simon said with very genuine cheerfulness.

He went to the door and opened it, revealing an excited-looking policeman—not the one he had first seen, who was still standing guard nearby—with a folded piece of paper in his hand.

"A message on the car radio, Inspector!" he said in rapid

French. "It concerns the identification of the dead man."

The policeman knew the message, and as he handed the paper to Inspector Edval he babbled a résumé of its contents. Vicky, who did not understand French, looked blank, while the Saint felt—if he did not actually look—positively beatified.

"Would you mind letting us foreigners in on the secret, Inspector?" Simon asked with halting humility. "After all, you're using my rather expensive room for your festivities."

Edval thought for a few seconds before answering. It was already obvious from a scorching glare he had shot at his uniformed subordinate that he had no faith whatever in the Saint's supposed lack of linguistic ability.

"Jaeger is not Jaeger," he said, seeming to take an unofficial poetic pleasure in the lilt of the words. Perhaps he was the sort of man who read Baudelaire secretly in bed. "Or perhaps I should say, he was both Jaeger and someone else —a former Gestapo agent named Norden who operated secretly in this country during the '39 war. We have rather complete files on such people, including dental charts and scars."

A transformation was taking place in Vicky's expression that was subtle but movingly complete. She met the police inspector's probing eyes directly as he turned to her.

"But you were about to tell me something, mademoiselle," he said. "And this further identification of the victim certainly does not decrease the chance that he might have been pushed out of a window."

"I can tell you that he wasn't pushed out of this window," Vicky replied in a completely confident voice. "At least not by Mr Templar. Mr Templar and I went out together, and there certainly wasn't any sign then that anybody had fallen anywhere."

"And when was that, mademoiselle?" Edval inquired.

"About a quarter to eight," Simon answered helpfully.

"I would prefer that the lady answer my questions," Edval said.

"About a quarter to eight," said Vicky.

Edval sighed.

"May I see your passport, please?"

Vicky opened her purse and produced the booklet. Edval bowed slightly as he took it. He looked at each page closely before speaking again.

"Very good, Mademoiselle Kinian. I suppose you are a good friend of Monsieur Templar?"

"I've only seen him once before in my life. We met in Lisbon when I first got there and found out we were both coming here—so we made a date."

She paused, and the Saint nodded acknowledgement.

"I'm a very lucky man, as you can see, Inspector," he said gallantly.

"I have heard of your remarkable luck," the inspector replied with some irony. "And this absence of yours this evening—this was because of your date?"

He spoke "date" with quotation marks around it, as a foreign word he found faintly distasteful and amusing.

"That's right," said Vicky.

Edval looked at his watch.

"It was not a very long date, was it?"

There was an edge of sarcasm on Simon's voice as he interrupted.

"I was aware of Swiss efficiency," he said, "but I never knew that it extended to timing the social engagements of tourists."

Inspector Edval compressed his lips and exercised self-control.

"My excuses if I have offended anyone." He handed the passport back to Vicky. "Thank you, mademoiselle. I do not see how I can doubt the testimony of a young lady with such a fresh new passport and such a charming and honest face."

"Thank you," she said, a little uncomfortably.

"I hope you will forgive me, too, for any insinuations, Monsieur Templar, but when the Saint is in the vicinity of any unusual happening it must be routine to make sure he is not connected with it."

"You are absolved," said the Saint benevolently. "Go, and my blessings be with you."

The inspector almost smiled, but covered his embarrassment at that near slip by mumbling a few final words about Jaeger as he went to the door.

"It is possible," he said, "that he was attempting to steal something, and fell to his death while trying to climb from one room to another outside the hotel."

"Of course! Why didn't *I* think of that?" Simon said with admiration. "I'm sure that if you follow up that theory you'll have the case closed in no time."

"*Merci,*" said Inspector Edval, and left.

Vicky collapsed into a chair and closed her eyes as Simon moved back from closing the door.

"Wonderful to watch the professional police mind at work, isn't it?" he commented.

"To think you've been going through this all your life," Vicky said. "I couldn't even take another day of it."

"And now I suppose you expect to be paid off for your part in this little drama we've just been through," the Saint said.

Vicky looked up at him.

"You don't have to be nasty about it," she said.

"I'm not being nasty," he replied. "I'm being practical."

Vicky got up from the chair, and as she talked she meandered with conspicuous inconspicuousness to the general area of the door through which Edval had made his exit.

"You think nobody does anything without an angle, don't you?" she asked huffily.

"Well, darling," Simon answered, "I'm much too modest to kid myself that you lied to that rather trusting Swiss Sherlock because you just suddenly fell in love with me."

"I should say not!" Vicky responded indignantly. "I guess it wouldn't occur to you that I might have felt an obligation to you—because even if you did knock Jaeger or Norden or whoever he was out of the window, it was only what I'd have wanted to do if I'd known who he really was."

"Maybe so," said the Saint. "But I'm also sure you realized you couldn't let me be pinched while I had this little package in my pocket."

She gave him credit for accurate divination by a moment of stymied silence.

"But anyway," she said belligerently, "you admit I got you out of a jam, so how about *your* obligation?"

The Saint was now lounging casually on the sofa with his long legs crossed in front of him, while the girl was still standing next to the closed door.

"First," he said, "may I ask why you're loitering over there on the threshold?"

"So I can get out in case you take it into your head to throw *me* out of the window!"

She tried to say it with the same sting that she had summoned a few seconds before.

"You forget what a mercenary pirate's mind I have," Simon said impudently. "I'd never toss a prize like you overboard—I'd sell you to the slave traders." As an afterthought he added, "Or keep you for myself."

Her eyes met Simon's roguish blue ones, and in the next moment she blushed, but looked completely reassured.

"You changed the subject," she said. "I've told you why I was standing by the door. Now you tell me what you intend to do about that stuff my father told *me* how to get."

"I'll take some convincing before I'm ready to admit that it belongs to either one of us. But first let's see what it is."

He pulled the thin packet from inside his coat and put it on the polished mahogany surface of the coffee table in front of the sofa where he was sitting. Vicky had lost her fear so completely that she came and sat next to him.

"I don't care who it belonged to," she said, "or what it is. I think I've earned a share of it."

"And so have I," he asserted. "So let's find out if there's enough in it for both of us—or if this is just one more of your father's boyish pranks."

He peeled off the adhesive tapes which secured the oil-cloth package and then began to unfold the black wrapping itself. Beside him, Vicky perched on the edge of her sofa cushion and clenched her hands together in tense excitement. Simon laid back the last fold of oilcloth. There in the middle lay a slightly oversized white envelope.

"Oh no!" Vicky groaned. "Not another one!"

She let herself flop back in the sofa, and her hands fell in limp despair at her sides.

"Next stop Bangkok or Tel Aviv," agreed the Saint. "It looks as if Dad has an almost inexhaustible sense of suspense—or maybe he figured that if he made the puzzle long enough anybody but a devoted blood-relative would give up long before he got to the end of the line."

"You won't want it, then," said Vicky.

As she spoke she moved with a suddenness and speed that would have given a jaguar twinges of envy. She pounced on the envelope, snatched it up, turned the coffee table over against the Saint's legs, and bolted for the door.

2

Before Vicky could get the door open the Saint had disengaged himself from the coffee-table obstacle she had thrown in his path and was halfway across the room after her. While she was still fumbling desperately with the lock he caught her, pinned her arms more or less at her sides with one of his arms, and tried to get the envelope out of her hand.

She struggled furiously, holding the envelope out of his reach behind her for as long as she could. Then his patiently applied superior strength paid off, and the envelope was once more in his possession.

"Trusting little soul, aren't you?" he remarked, still gripping her firmly. "Trustworthy, too."

Vicky squirmed helplessly and winced with rage.

"Anybody would be crazy to trust you, you . . . you rattlesnake!"

Simon clucked sadly and released his hold on her.

"It pains me to think that you could turn on your friend, counsellor, and protector like this, at a moment which I'd have thought would be marked by joyful gratitude and adoring thanks."

"You'll keep it all for yourself!" she said accusingly, rubbing her arm where he had gripped it.

"I gather you have some advance dope on the contents of this little prize package that you haven't shared with your faithful comrade. In that case you may not be inquisitive enough to want to stick around for the grand opening --so please feel free to leave."

"No!" she snapped. "It's more mine than anybody's, and I'm going to get it, no matter what you say!"

Simon was strolling back towards the sofa again, tapping

the bulging sealed envelope against the palm of one hand, and then suddenly he turned and took a threatening step towards her.

"You may get a quick trip through that window after all if you don't mind your manners," he said ferociously.

She gave a terrified squeak and jumped back towards the door. But she turned again at bay, clinging to the handle.

"You come one step closer and I'll start screaming. I bet Edval's still got a man outside. And you know whose word they'll take when I start talking."

The Saint dissolved into helpless laughter.

"We really should take this act on the road," he chortled. "However, to play it straight for a minute, let's pretend that we each have the other over a barrel, which is not a state of affairs conducive to progress in any direction. Shall we declare a truce and get on with our nefarious huddle?"

She relaxed a little but did not step forward at once.

"You're not getting me anywhere near that window," she insisted defensively.

"And I'm not letting you anywhere near this table or any other flingable furniture," he told her. "Maybe we'll have to meet from now on in a padded cell."

He righted the table with the toe of his shoe and stripped open the envelope. It yielded a thick wad of papers. Unfolding them, he saw that there were six sheets, each almost identical to the others, but each addressed—in German—to a different bank. The names of the different cities in which the banks were located first caught his eye: Lisbon, Buenos Aires, Caracas, Madrid, Zürich, Johannesburg. Then something else attracted his attention: the sum of money held in each bank to which the letters of credit in his hand pertained. The amounts were expressed in various currencies, but quick mental calculation reduced each of them to approximately the same astonishing sum.

The Saint was accustomed to cash in large figures, having

a useful quantity of it stashed away in his own accounts, so the fact that he blinked, looked in amazement at Vicky, and then stared reverently down again at the papers was a high tribute to the grandeur of their contents.

"Do you know what we've got here?" he said.

"Letters of credit," Vicky replied, still a little coldly. "My father's letter told me that, but he never saw them and didn't know how much they were worth."

"They are worth," Simon said, "ten million dollars each."

"*Ten . . . million . . . dollars?*"

To render typographically the awesome quality Vicky gave to each of her next words would require a surface the size of the north face of the Eiger and the labor of a few hundred sign painters working all summer with no time off.

"Yes," Simon confirmed simply.

"*Each?*" she squealed.

"Yes."

She forgot all about the possibility of an enforced exit through the window and rushed to his side, gaping at the documents over his shoulder.

"How many are there?"

"Six," he answered. "Six worth ten million bucks each, no questions asked, to anyone who fills in his name and signature and takes it to the bank it's addressed to."

Vicky absorbed the information in silence for a while, and then sighed in a masterpiece of inadequacy: "My goodness!"

"Mine too," said the Saint. "Virtue is about to be rewarded once more, it seems, thanks to pluck, perseverance, and all the other old-fashioned nobilities—not to mention greed and your father."

He shuffled the letters about on the table, arranging and re-arranging them in random geometrical patterns, while he continued to digest the full flavor of the prize with ripening rapture. Seldom in the history of buccaneering could any pirate have doodled with such precious playthings: never had he himself held so much concentrated capital in his hands all at once.

And besides the pure crass opulence of the booty, there were its artistic implications to enjoy: the inspiration which had hit upon such a supremely simple method of caching a Golconda so that anyone who knew the secret could claim it without revealing any past names or identifications, the ingenuity which had devised such an improbable safe deposit for the claim checks, even the macabre humour which had selected for the ultimate depository a miniature casket bearing such a name as Josef Meier. And to top that, the fact that the evil men who had put away such an insurance policy for their own uncertain future had never survived to cash it, whereas one of their victims had been able to ensure that it was at least not lost for ever.

Vicky Kinian said: "My father was risking his life for his country as a soldier, and I know he wouldn't have betrayed it for any amount of money. But this must have seemed like something quite apart from winning the war. Whoever got this money, so long as it wasn't the Nazis, it wouldn't have hurt our side. Somehow, he found out about it and had a chance to leave it to me instead of getting it turned over to the Government. I honestly can't blame him for being tempted."

"You shouldn't blame me either, then," Simon averred.

She looked worried.

"Any more than I should blame you," he concluded.

She seemed a little relieved.

"What are we going to do?" she asked.

"I propose to keep one of these for my services—and please don't embarrass both of us by telling me you can't spare it."

He separated the Johannesburg letter from the stack and handed the other five sheets to Vicky. Her face was white and her fingers trembled so much that the papers rustled loudly. She sank down on the sofa, gazed uncomprehendingly at the typed text of the documentary forms, and hugged them close against her body.

She looked up at Simon, hardly able to speak.

"So you think I'm entitled to this money?"

The Saint had already tucked his personal dividend into his pocket.

"Maybe," he said thoughtfully. "But unfortunately I'm not the one who'll decide whether to let you keep it. One can assume that the happy Aryans who stashed it away got it by some unsavory or illegitimate means, but where did they embezzle it or which individuals did they rob? That could keep an army of lawyers busy for another twenty years." He sat down in a chair facing her, rested his elbows on the arms, and folded his hands underneath his chin as he considered the problem. "Remember, I'm in on this hunt because some lads in the Pentagon asked me to solve the mystery of your father and report what I could find out. If Washington releases the information, there are going to be more claimants for this dough than bees in a clover patch."

Vicky was beginning to look more defiant than worried.

"I don't see how any of them could prove they've any right to it!" she said. "How could anybody else have found it?"

"I doubt that anybody could, but both of us would be far beyond caring by the time the legal weasels finish gnawing the bones."

"So you mean I've got a choice between being a sort of thief and being broke for the rest of my life," Vicky said sulkily. "Assuming *you* give me any choice at all. I notice you've already got your share safely tucked away. I'm the only one who'll be sitting around waiting for my reward for the next eighty years."

Simon picked up the remaining five letters of credit and spread them like playing cards in his hands.

"Well, just in case the authorities aren't properly grateful, I guess it's only fair that you should have a little something to tide you over while they embroider the red tape." He selected the letter addressed to the Zürich bank and passed it to her. "There. Sweets for the sweet. We can say there were only four letters—which, as anybody can plainly see, there are."

He placed the four sheets of paper back on the table and noted the ambivalent look Vicky was giving them.

"Don't be so sad," he said. "Ten million dollars is more than you're ever likely to spend, and if you had the rest you could only bequeath it to the care of indigent wombats or the restoration of ancient Egyptian outhouses."

"I'd still rather decide what happens to it than let a lot of bureaucrats get their hands on it!" she protested.

"I'd rather you did too, but I've got to maintain a few of my personally tailored ethics or I'd never get invited to nice people's homes."

He folded the four papers and put them in one of his pockets separate from the letter he had reserved for himself.

"And how do I know what you'll do with those?" Vicky asked suspiciously.

"Come with me to the American Embassy, if you like, and watch me hand them in," he answered without hesitation. "In fact, you'd better stick to me like a burr till tomorrow. If there are any other treasure-hunters left, they may realize they've got to get us before the banks open in the morning. In fact, any life insurance that'll do us any good will only take effect when the Ungodly are convinced that all the loot is out of our hands."

Vicky, who had been in the process of putting her own

letter in her purse, suddenly stopped and looked up again at Simon.

"I never thought of that," she said in a hushed voice. "Do you really think there might be others? I just assumed we'd finished with them."

"Well, your boyfriend Jaeger didn't strike me as the type to share his toys with his friends, but it's possible that he wasn't working alone. And assuming that Graveyard Mischa isn't a free-lance ghoul, he may have been working with Jaeger or with some equally unwholesome party—perhaps Soviet in origin, judging by his name. I don't want to make you nervous, but if we live to eat lunch tomorrow that in itself will be something to celebrate."

Vicky snapped her bag shut and stared at the Saint's calm face with wide eyes.

"Oh, no, you don't make me nervous," she said shakily. "You just make me petrified."

"A little dose of caution wouldn't hurt you a bit," he said. "And a little dose of strong drink wouldn't hurt either of us. Scotch is all I've got in stock. Is that all right?"

Vicky nodded numbly.

"Straight," she said.

Simon poured each of them a dollop of Peter Dawson and added ice from the melting supply in a bucket on his dressing table.

"I think you must have cat blood," he said over his shoulder to his subdued guest. "Even so, you must be down to your seventh or eighth life by now. I'd suggest a long and pleasure-rich retirement far from scenes of international intrigue and strife."

"You'd never believe it," she said, "but in Des Moines I'd have been scared to take a bus alone at night. I don't know what came over me to give me the nerve to do what I've done on this trip."

Simon handed her a glass and raised his to her in a casual toast.

"Whatever it is, here's to it," he said. "And if you'll pardon the analogy, since there's no resemblance to you whatsoever in shape, here's to all the broomstraws who've found they can drive straight through a solid oak door in a strong wind."

Vicky smiled and drank, meeting his eyes with really human warmth for the first time since they had met.

"I'm sorry I've been so—"

Her sentence was cut off by a series of precisely spaced knocks at the door. Vicky blanched, and Simon got to his feet.

"Just stay where you are," he said quietly.

He was ready for anything when he unlocked the door and partially opened it, but he was not called upon to resist any violent onslaughts. There in the hallway, looking as harmless as an overfed guinea pig, stood only a shortish plump man with a bald head and a white Vandyke beard.

3

"And what can we do for you?" inquired the Saint courteously.

He stood blocking the door, and his bespectacled caller, dressed in a slightly rumpled dove-grey suit of vaguely outmoded cut, held out an identity card encased in clear plastic.

"I hope you recognize this," the man said quietly. "It is not often shown."

"As a matter of fact," Simon said with equal smoothness before looking at the card, "I recognize *you*. Didn't we bump into one another on the stairs of a hotel in Lisbon?"

"It is more than possible," the stranger said.

There was no trace of a smile or any other softening of his stolid face. The Saint looked at the card and turned to speak to Vicky.

"Mr Boris Uzdanov of Uncle Sam's CIA . . . or so it says," he told her.

"I would like to come out of the corridor," Uzdanov said with a trace of uneasiness. "Do you mind? You may search me if you wish. I am not armed." He lifted the wooden cane he carried in his right hand. "Unless of course you count this."

Simon nodded and stood aside. He felt sure he could deal with the visitor's cane, whatever unadvertised qualities it might possess.

Uzdanov stepped into the room and made a perfunctory bow in Vicky's direction as the door was closed behind him. He produced another identity card.

"Shall I continue with business?" he asked. "Time is not a thing I have much of at the moment."

"By all means," the Saint agreed. "None of us is suffering from a surplus."

"As this card tells you, I am also a member of the local communist organization, which I was able to infiltrate, and an occasional agent of the MVD—luckily for you, Mr Templar."

The confessed double agent blinked through his spectacles as he awaited a reaction.

"I'm most gratified to hear about my good fortune," murmured Simon. "Do I need to ask which of those superspy outfits is likely to end up with the honour of paying your old age pension?"

Uzdanov bridled perceptibly, but his rather breathy hushed voice was unaffected.

"I assure you that my loyalty is to the West. My superiors

in Washington are perfectly satisfied of that. My family were murdered by the Red Army in the Ukraine."

Vicky looked reproachfully at Simon, who made a gesture that invited Uzdanov to go on with his explanations.

"Since I am Russian, the CIA has naturally tended to use me for work involving Soviet activities, and in the course of my everyday work I happened to find out that our friends in the Kremlin had heard rumours of the Nazi money Miss Kinian was looking for."

Vicky was awestricken.

"You mean they heard about *me?*" she gasped. "In Moscow?"

"That is correct," said Uzdanov formally. "Just as the American intelligence services knew about you—and just as the ex-Gestapo man Norden knew about you."

Vicky sank back into her chair as if she might disappear entirely, an event which apparently would not have displeased her in the least.

"I think I'm going to faint," she croaked.

"It does sound as if you've had about as much private life as a bug under a microscope," Simon admitted.

"You say the nicest things."

Uzdanov obviously had no penchant for idle badinage.

"You are fortunate to be alive, indeed, Miss Kinian. It was an MVD man who attacked you tonight . . ."

Vicky looked at him sharply.

"You know that? How . . ."

Uzdanov raised an authoritative hand and interrupted.

"Directly it was known that Ruspine had failed to get the funds after his visit to the cemetery tonight, I was ordered to impersonate a Swiss detective, arrest both of you, and take you into a trap."

"And the Russians would do all that just for . . . a little money?" Vicky asked.

The Saint met her glance with a warning look which should have reduced her to silence.

"They were interested enough to have ordered me to kill Ruspine if he failed," Uzdanov told her. "It was an assignment which I found it quite humorous to carry out."

"*You* murdered him?" Vicky gulped.

"Why not? The CIA surely couldn't object to my accommodating the Kremlin by eliminating one of their own agents at their own request."

"And I suppose Ruspine was expected to find enough loot to repay the effort," Simon prompted him.

"The Soviets can use funds of that kind to finance their operations abroad," Uzdanov said. "But I'm afraid I have very little time to explain everything now. I am expected to take you from the hotel, pretending to have you under arrest, and to deliver you to communist agents within the half-hour. Of course I had already had word from Colonel Wade in Lisbon to keep an eye out for you, Mr Templar. So you see, I am now in a most awkward position. I can hardly turn you over to the MVD, but if I do not . . ."

His stubby hands made a gesture of futility on either side of his paunch.

The Saint was still watching him closely, trying to estimate just how much showed above the water and how much still bobbed below the depths. He had remembered immediately on opening his door that the white-bearded man who stood there was the same one who had been dawdling in the Geneva airport terminal earlier in the day. Uzdanov had said that he had been ordered to keep an eye out for the Saint, but he had only offhandedly admitted being on the Tagus Hotel stairs in Lisbon and had not even mentioned his presence in the Geneva airport lobby—a fact Simon had deliberately avoided bringing up. Nevertheless, the Saint knew better than most people how devious the reticences and evasions of an undercover operator must sometimes be. Now he decided to make a small test.

"I can understand your position," he said easily. "I just wish you'd been able to get in touch with me when I first got to Geneva before lunch . . ."

Suddenly the other's dark eyes were riveted on him. There was almost no interval before Uzdanov spoke.

"You are joking with me?" he challenged in return.

"How?"

"You came to Geneva this afternoon—and you waited for a time in the terminal building. I know. I was there watching you."

"I know," Simon said blandly. "I was watching you."

Uzdanov continued to study him detachedly. Then, with a kind of impatient frustration, he tugged at his white beard.

"You still don't trust me," he said.

"I'm more inclined to believe you now than I was before," the Saint responded. "But if you're going to suggest that we should play rats to even a CIA Pied Piper, I'm afraid we can't oblige."

"Of course not," Uzdanov said. "It's obviously out of the question that I turn you over to the communists—"

"Then what's the problem?" Simon demanded. "Miss Kinian and I were just going to slide out of here in a hurry anyhow. If you tell the comrades we'd already disappeared when you got to the hotel . . ."

"It is not quite so easy," Uzdanov interjected. "Like Mischa Ruspine, I too am watched. If you leave now you will be seen, and if I leave without you, everything I have built up for several years will be exploded—even if nothing worse happens to me. The consequences for you could also be violent." He took a few nervous paces as he talked and then faced the Saint again. "We must leave together, making it look as if I had carried out my orders. Then, after we have shaken off any followers, you will overpower me and escape—perhaps leaving a bump on my skull just to keep the performance convincing."

Vicky looked at Simon anxiously. His expression was much more solemn than she had ever seen it before. Inside his head arguments and counterarguments traded thrusts with dizzying speed. When all advantages and disadvantages, threats and possible parries had been weighed, one overwhelming fact remained: Boris Uzdanov was on his hands, and there was no really uncomplicated way to get rid of him—whether his story was genuine or not—here at the hotel. Friend or foe, to ditch him now could easily bring on an immediate crisis.

"Okay, we'll play it your way," the Saint said at last, with abrupt decisiveness. "It'll get us out of here—and we can hope it saves blowing your cover."

Uzdanov's stocky body relaxed a little and his lips showed, for the first time, that they were capable of flexing into some semblance of a heartfelt smile.

"I'm delighted," he said. "It is by far the best way to handle this business. I shall now escort you out the front door of the hotel, according to my instructions."

"And into a waiting Black Maria supplied by the same firm that made your Swiss police identity card?" Simon asked.

"One must improvise." Uzdanov shrugged. "We can take a taxi."

"Where to?"

They were all on their feet now, and Uzdanov looked at his pocket watch.

"It doesn't matter," he said. "We can think of a way to shake off anyone who is following me once we are out of the hotel."

Simon shook his head.

"It might be easier if we take my car. It's parked in front of the hotel already."

"That would be even better," said Uzdanov.

"Fine. Let's get the chain gang on the road, then."

The Saint opened the door of his room cautiously, saw that there was nobody in the hall, and motioned for Uzdanov and Vicky to go out ahead of him.

"You must go first," Uzdanov said. "An arresting officer cannot walk in front of the parties he is arresting."

"Quite right," Simon assented reluctantly.

He put his arm around Vicky's waist and ushered her into the corridor ahead of him.

"And how does an arrested party walk?" she whispered.

"With a worried expression," he replied helpfully.

"I can guarantee that," she said.

"There is no need to be nervous," Uzdanov assured them. "I am the one who will end up with a lump on the head. It is better than a bullet in the back of the neck, which is what I would get if my idealistic and peace-loving comrades knew what I was doing."

They had reached the elevator, which responded quickly to the Saint's push of the down button. The cabin, like the corridor, was unoccupied, and the swift ride to ground level took place in silence.

"Now," Simon said as the door slid open. "Look possessive, Detective Uzdanov, and Miss Kinian and I will look obedient."

He took Vicky's arm, and the two of them preceded the Russian across the lobby and through the main doors without attracting any attention among the few other people in the area. Outside, the sidewalk was deserted. The doorman had retired for the night, and the taxi drivers who earlier in the evening had waited in their cabs outside the hotel had now either gone off duty or moved to more lively parts of town.

"My car's over there," Simon said, taking Vicky's arm.

"I don't see anybody watching us," she said in a low voice.

"In that doorway," the Saint indicated, in a similar undertone.

Vicky's eyes followed the direction of his glance and picked out the shadowy forms of two men, one in a beret, conversing on the steps of a building across the street.

"They don't seem at all interested in us," she said.

"And maybe they aren't," Simon conceded noncommittally. "But they may be a couple of little droplets in the Wave of the Future."

They had reached his hired car.

"I will get in the back," Uzdanov said. "I suggest that Mr Templar drive and you sit next to him, Miss Kinian."

"Correct procedure again," the Saint approved.

A moment later they were all inside the car.

"So far so good?" Vicky asked.

Uzdanov darted a look in the direction of the men in the doorway.

"Yes," he said. "It should look as if I have been able to follow my instructions exactly. This, of course, is how we would sit if I were trying to control two possibly dangerous prisoners."

"A thoroughly professional job, up to this point," the Saint said. "Now what?"

"Drive," Uzdanov suggested simply.

Simon started the engine.

"I don't suppose anybody cares which way I go?" he inquired.

"How about Iowa?" Vicky proposed with a nervous shiver.

"Straight ahead," Uzdanov said. "We must make it appear that we are going to the rendezvous where I was told to bring you."

"Clear enough," said Simon. "Straight ahead it is."

He put the car into gear and accelerated away from the curb. He was so quickly out of the circle in front of the Hotel Portal that he had no chance to see whether the ostensible loafers in the doorway had moved or not.

"Which of your nursemaids is likely to follow us?" he asked.

"I would like to know that myself," Uzdanov answered.

He was leaning forward, looking between Vicky and Simon at the road ahead.

"If I keep on going straight ahead we'll end up in the lake," the Saint said mildly. "Are your pals in a submarine?"

"Turn left at the next corner," Uzdanov said humourlessly. "Then take the next fork on the left and follow that road for some time."

Simon obeyed the instructions. They merged into a major thoroughfare leading out of town, but at that hour of the night there was little concentrated traffic, and as far as he could tell in the rear-view mirror there were no cars within a hundred yards or more behind him.

"Your chums don't seem to be very efficient," he remarked to the Russian in the back seat.

"How do you mean?" Uzdanov asked.

"That was the easiest job of losing a tail I've ever been through."

Uzdanov turned and studied the road through the back window.

"Perhaps we have lost them. Perhaps not. Perhaps they are now satisfied that we are going to the place where I was ordered to take you. In any case, I would never underestimate them. By letting a man know that he *may* be watched all the time they can afford to cut corners occasionally and let fear do the job for them."

"It does save on petrol," Simon acknowledged. "What now?"

"Continue," said Uzdanov.

After another eight or ten minutes, while he was still turned away from the front seat of the car pretending to watch the road for followers, he surreptitiously closed the strong short fingers of his right hand around the curved handle of his cane and gave it a twist. With an almost imperceptible click it loosened, and with deliberate precaution against any rasp of metal he drew the handle away from the cane. The slim metal shaft of the hidden dagger emerged, inch by inch, its polished steel flaring in the light of street lamps passing overhead.

Vicky Kinian suddenly turned and looked back over her shoulder, and Uzdanov hunched to hide the detached dagger below the back of the front seat.

"Is there anybody behind us that you can see?" she asked.

To Uzdanov's relief she was looking past his head and through the rear window at the road, where traffic was becoming more and more sparse as the Volkswagen moved out of the city towards the hill country to the northeast.

"I see nobody," Uzdanov said. He pretended to scrutinize the receding highway, all the while huddling over the hollow and the lethal halves of his cane. "I think we can assume we are alone. In a minute we will make another turn."

Vicky faced front again.

"Now all we have to do is think of how we overpower you," she said.

Uzdanov turned forward.

"That will not be a problem," he said comfortably. He raised his needle-pointed stiletto to the level of the nape of Vicky's neck. "I have changed my mind about being overpowered."

4

"You will continue to obey my orders," Uzdanov said, "or I shall be forced to cut Miss Kinian's throat."

He suddenly leaned a little farther forward, and Vicky screamed and automatically jerked away from the point of the knife that touched her neck, shrinking against the door on her side. The Saint, steering a small car that was zipping along a dark highway at seventy miles an hour, could only continue to keep a steady hold on the wheel and try desperately from the corners of his eyes to see what was happening beside and behind him.

Uzdanov's hand guided the edge of his dagger around the skin of Vicky's throat without once giving her a serious chance of escaping it. In the circumstances it was a tribute to his skill in the use of his favorite weapon that he managed to keep her under direct threat without accidentally stabbing into her jugular vein.

"Do not move any more!" he commanded her sternly. "Absolutely do not move!"

She froze, rigid with terror, and only her eyes disobeyed the Russian, rolling to stare pleadingly at Simon, who cursed himself for having relaxed his guard enough to let such a thing happen. His fault was not so much that he had trusted Uzdanov—the amount of trust he had felt could have been measured in fractions of a grain—but that he had trusted himself too completely. In this case, self-assurance had been a more dangerous enemy than any cleverness on Uzdanov's part.

Uzdanov, however, did not see it that way. He gloated as he held the knife to Vicky's throat and the car hurtled on through the darkness.

"It was so obliging of you to fall for the very story which

I thought was most likely to disarm your suspicions! Now—"

He cut himself short as they rounded a curve in the road and began to overtake a policeman on a motorcycle.

"Hullo!" Simon said cheerfully. "An escort."

"Do not stop!" the Russian warned. "Keep up a normal speed until I tell you to turn. If you try anything at all, Templar, this girl is dead!"

The Volkswagen sped around the motorcycle policeman, who was cruising along at about forty-five miles an hour. Very gradually, Simon eased the pressure of his foot on his car's accelerator pedal, keeping the cyclops-light of the motorcycle in view behind him; but the subterfuge was more mechanical than optimistic.

"You are slowing down!" Uzdanov said implacably. "Get back up to a hundred kilometres. Soon we come to a crossroad. Take the right-hand road, where the signpost says Lausanne."

Ahead was a cluster of houses, only two or three with lights in their windows, grouped around the dividing point of the highway. The Saint followed the instructions, and Uzdanov grunted with satisfaction as the car moved out into more uninhabited countryside.

The terrain became much more mountainous, and the road curved around the contours of wooded slopes. There were few lights within sight of the highway, and no traffic.

"Now," the Russian said, "before I tell you what to do next, let me warn you not to try to throw me off balance with any sudden turns. You would be much more likely to cause damage to Miss Kinian than to me."

Uzdanov's breath was on the Saint's neck, and the fist that held the dagger against Vicky's throat was tantalizingly near Simon's shoulder. Slowly the Saint slid his own right hand to a point on the steering wheel that would give him the best angle for a surprise attack on the Russian, but Uzdanov was a well-trained and observant man.

"If you try to grab for my hand you can be *sure* Miss Kinian will be very badly hurt," he said unemotionally.

The Saint was forming a plan, the first stage of which was to use the Russian's strategy in reverse—to throw the man off his guard with a pretence of surrender. Obviously any sort of desperate lunge had to be ruled out.

"Well, congratulations, chum," he said with a sigh of resignation. "I thought I was too old to buy any of the standard cock-and-bull stories, but you certainly sold one."

"You need not feel too foolish, Templar. It is an axiom of the Party that any man can be duped if the right psychology is applied."

"And I suppose you really are a Party member in good standing."

"Of course. But by admitting it from the start, while at the same time presenting myself as a CIA agent, I disarmed your suspicions before they could form."

"Thank you, teacher," said the Saint. "And what's the next dazzling move you have in mind? I'd suggest something fairly brilliant, since the head porter saw us leave the hotel together. If anything funny happens to this innocent American tourist and me he's sure to give the police your description."

Uzdanov either chuckled or choked slightly, producing an unmusical nasal sound which for him conceivably had connotations of mirth.

"I would not count on his help if I were you, Templar. He also happens to be a member of the Party. He will remember nothing about you or this—" Uzdanov snorted congestively again. "This innocent tourist! Or he will remember whatever I tell him to." Then his voice became more harsh and business-like. "Now, I want to see one of those letters that you were preparing to share between you."

"Letters?" Simon repeated innocently. "The only thing we were preparing to share was a bottle of Peter Dawson."

Suddenly Vicky gave a little wincing sort of cry. With sickness deep in his stomach, the Saint knew that Uzdanov had used his knife.

"I only hurt her a little that time, Templar, but if you joke with me I won't be so lenient again. Put on the overhead light, Miss Kinian, take the letter from your purse, open it, and hold it up so I can see it over your shoulder."

Vicky moved with terrorized slowness to obey his commands. As she switched on the light above her door Simon could see a tiny trickle of blood beside her chin, like a dark fracture in the otherwise flawless moulding of her face. The car was moving up a steep hill. On one side was a wall of rock rising directly up from the side of the pavement, and on the other side was a sheer precipice dropping away into the darkness of the valley below, where a feeble constellation of lights showed the location of some sleeping village.

"Are you hurt much?" Simon asked over the deepening drone of the straining engine.

"No," Vicky answered with desperate calm.

"Do exactly as he says from now on," the Saint told her quietly. "He's got us, I'm afraid. Apparently the Party also furnishes X-ray eyes for its higher-echelon agents."

"X-ray ears, you might say," Uzdanov amended. "I overheard your discussion with a listening device just before I knocked on your door. Now, Miss Kinian, hold the letter up . . . Yes. Good."

Uzdanov scanned the sheet in silence as the Volkswagen labored on towards the top of the steep grade up which it had been laboring for the past five minutes; then without warning his free hand darted forward and snatched the letter of credit out of Vicky's fingers.

"Thank you," he said. "I see that my search is finished."

"And so are we if your plans continue on schedule—is that right, Mr Ooze-enough?" Simon asked.

The Russian re-asserted his domination over them by

pressing the point of his stiletto close against the side of Vicky's neck. He ignored the Saint's question.

"I heard you discussing five other letters before I knocked on your door, Templar. Pass them to me, please, but continue to drive at the same speed."

"And what happens if we go on tamely doing what you tell us, commissar?"

"Nothing worse, eventually, than a long walk back to town. You will be of no further importance, and I shall be on my way."

"But that's only what applied psychology tells you to say," Simon argued evenly. "If we knew we'd be killed anyhow, which I suspect is to be the high point of this conducted promenade, we wouldn't have any reason to obey you at all, would we?"

"Your only hope is that I may not hurt either of you if you give me no trouble. You must simply cling to that. Now, give me the letters!"

"I'm sorry, Vicky," said the Saint wearily. "You might have done better if I'd let you alone."

His uncharacteristic modesty was one more attempt to relax Uzdanov's guard; but whether there was really any chance of swinging the balance away from the Russian was a question that only the next agonizing minutes could decide.

"Hurry up!" Uzdanov snapped as Simon took his time pulling the letters from inside his jacket. "And why are you slowing down?"

"The horses are getting tired," Simon explained. "But we'll try to oblige you. I think the rest of the trip will be downhill."

The car had reached the crest, and a road sign indicated a steep curvaceous descent for the next several kilometres. As Simon produced the letters, but still being careful to keep them out of Uzdanov's reach, the Volkswagen began to purr with relief as it built up speed on the first downhill stretch.

"Two can play the carrot-and-the-stick game, comrade," Simon said in a tone that had new firmness in it. "Don't do anything hasty—and cling to the hope that I won't drop these." He thrust the letters out the window, clutching them at arm's length, as he steered the car with his right hand only. "If I let them go, that's fifty million dollars that may not land this side of Lake Como."

Uzdanov was considerably less calm than he had been a few seconds before, and his voice shifted into a new hysterical key that made the extent of his discomfiture pleasantly unmistakeable.

"Bring those letters inside or I'll kill her!" he yowled.

The Saint's voice was more placid in precisely inverse ratio to the raised pitch of Uzdanov's.

"You'd better not hurt her, because then I wouldn't care what I did."

The car's speed was up to sixty now, and the wind tore at the papers in the Saint's hand. They seemed alive and fighting to be free. Uzdanov ground his teeth audibly and switched the aim of his stiletto from Vicky's throat to the back of the Saint's neck.

"I think you must care what happens to yourself!" he shouted. "Bring those letters inside!"

"Don't make me nervous, pal, or I might run over a cliff. In this kind of country the man at the wheel has to keep his mind on the road, and of all the back-seat drivers I've ever had the misfortune to travel with, you're the most distracting."

Simon could feel the point of Uzdanov's knife against his skin, squarely in the centre of the back of his neck. One slip and the blade could plunge forward through flesh and bone, severing the connection of spinal cord and brain stem. But at least he felt sure that his enemy would not sink the dagger into him on purpose at the moment, since the consequences for the Russian would have been as disastrous as for himself.

The car was careening down into the darkness at a hundred and twenty kilometres on a narrow road that seemed to writhe like a living reptile around the side of the mountain. Rubber shrieked against paving as the tires skidded through turn after turn. Simon dreaded the possibility of a curve so tight that he would be forced to slow down enough to allow Uzdanov to risk driving the knife into his neck and grabbing for the wheel himself.

But so far luck was on the Saint's side. The curves were hair-raising but banked enough to let him keep up a good speed, and as long as that lasted Uzdanov would be forced to wait.

Simon pulled the Volkswagen out of a particularly stomach-twirling loop, and said breezily: "We could all sing songs, I suppose. Anything to while away a dull trip. Why don't you teach us the *Internationale?*"

"Templar!" screamed Uzdanov impotently.

"Oooh," Vicky moaned.

She was leaning forward, clutching the handgrip on the dashboard as if to brace herself in case of a crash.

"Vicky, get down on the floor where he can't reach you!" Simon told her in a suddenly sharp voice. "Now!"

She scrambled off her seat and huddled in the narrow space under the dashboard on her side of the car, ready to fend off Uzdanov with her leather purse if he tried to lean over and take a jab at her.

"Don't try anything," the Saint ordered her. "Just keep away from that pig-sticker of his."

"What about *you?*" she cried.

"I've got him in the palm of my hand—can't you see?" Simon replied brightly. "I think he may be ready to make a deal. Is that right, Boris?"

To increase the impact of his words he jammed his foot down on the accelerator with a vehemence that seemed certain to send the car shooting straight out into space.

"Slow down!" Uzdanov screeched in a panic as the Volkswagen lurched into another bend.

"I thought you were the one who got such a kick out of speed," drawled the Saint.

Uzdanov's face must have achieved an expression of particular ferocity at that moment; Vicky, looking back at him, whimpered: "He'll kill you, Simon!"

"If he tries making shish kebab out of me he'll end up in the sauce himself, because we'll all three be taking a half-mile short-cut—straight down!"

Uzdanov cleared his throat as the car sailed down a relatively straight stretch. The needle-sharp point of his stiletto was as firmly as ever against Simon's neck.

"Perhaps . . . we can bargain," he said hoarsely.

"For a start you can throw that bodkin out of the window," the Saint told him. "Somehow I don't enjoy talking business when a strip of steel may be poking between my vertebrae at any second."

"No!" Uzdanov retorted. "You think I'm crazy? Slow down first, and then I will throw away the knife."

"In that case, I can see the three of us meandering along the road of life like this for ever," Simon said unconcernedly.

Wind whistled through the windows as the car zoomed on down the mountainside. The Russian grunted, obviously at a loss for any new form of persuasion. But while the deadlock was complete, it was becoming apparent that it could only be temporary.

"Sooner or later you will *have* to slow down, Templar," he said, with a gradual recovery of much of his former composure. "In the meantime, there is nothing you can do—and I can wait."

The Saint riposted with a blasé insouciance that was deliberately meant to be infuriating.

"When I do have to slow down, chum, it'll probably be because of traffic or a village cop—which'll be no time for you to start slaughtering your fellow-passengers. The dome light will still be on, remember, which will give you about as much privacy for your butchering as a goldfish in a public aquarium."

Uzdanov was not a man to be easily discouraged, nor to let trivia stand in his way.

"The light does not have to be on," he said.

As he leaned to one side and reached for the switch, to clinch his argument, Simon could feel the welcome detachment of the dagger's point from direct contact with his flesh.

This was the moment he had planned for, to which all his verbal sparring had been subtly directed.

Now he suddenly shifted his foot from the accelerator to the brake pedal. He could only hope that the knife was not poised directly behind him.

"Thanks, sucker," he said simultaneously. "Now I *will* slow down!"

He jammed his foot down, virtually freezing the rear wheels of the automobile on the spot. Uzdanov, off balance and without his unarmed hand to brace himself, was catapulted forward, his dagger stabbing past the Saint's head. Simon ducked as the sliver of steel shot past his jaw, and then he straightened galvanically up again like a released spring, smashing the back of his head into Uzdanov's face with something very close to the force and effect of a cannon ball.

VI: How Simon Templar continued
to be Helpful.

The Saint had no time to appreciate the devastation his skull had inflicted on Uzdanov's physiognomy. The sudden grab of the brakes had made the car swerve wildly and had hurled the Russian so violently forward that he might have continued on through the windshield if he had not been brought to a halt by Simon's head. He went heavily limp across the Saint's shoulders, his dagger clattering down among the foot controls, one of his forearms thrust between the spokes of the steering wheel, and the Saint struggled for control of the wheel as the car skidded with a scream of scorching rubber. Out of the corner of his eye he could see Vicky still balled on the floor next to his feet, her own eyes squeezed tightly shut. She let out a terrified gasp as she felt the car veer.

"Stay where you are!" Simon told her.

Somehow he kept the Volkswagen on the road in a swerving course that allowed no more sharp applications of the brake. It was all he could do to hold the car on the steep downgrade while he used all the leverage of his back to shrug and push the unconscious Uzdanov away, disengaging his fat arm from the steering wheel and dumping him off his shoulders and neck into the rear of the car.

As the Russian slid heavily back on to the floor behind, Simon had a more urgent problem to monopolize his attention. The headlights of the car, spearing out into the darkness, suddenly showed nothing at all. A hairpin turn was going its own way directly to the left, threatening to leave the Volkswagen with no more support under its wheels than several hundred feet of fresh and very dark mountain air. The Swiss highway authorities had reckoned that the bend could be negotiated at fifty kilometres an hour and had put up a sign marking it safe at forty. The Saint had just entered into it at a speed of almost eighty.

Only the instincts and skill of a Monte Carlo Rally driver, combined with a favorable nod from whatever gods concern themselves with such crises in the wee hours of the night, could have saved the car and its occupants from a graceful but rapidly drooping trajectory straight off the side of a cliff. By some miraculous combination of just the right amount of pressure on the brake and precise turns of the steering wheel Simon persuaded the car to keep its smoking tires more or less on the pavement.

A ton and more of metal responded to his delicate touch like a living thing. The highway and the rough shoulder to which it clung were a heaving blur as the machine, in a final fantastic pirouette, swung its engine-heavy rear to the fore with a wail like a riot of bagpipes. A partial spin had finally been the Saint's only choice. Any other end to his manoeuvres would have sent him rolling over the low safety wall and plummeting into the valley below.

The car slid to a crashing stop, half on and half off the road. The engine stalled and died, and suddenly the world seemed terribly quiet. There was a sensation of extreme remoteness, and the only sound was the wind, which strangely made the car seem to sway and quiver.

Simon sat very still, his senses acutely tuned to judge the extent of the Volkswagen's continuing predicament. It was not just vertigo or imagination which told him that the brisk Alpine breeze was making the car quiver. Straight ahead of him from where he sat in the driver's seat, the car's headlights illuminated the sheer wall of rock which rose straight up from the inner side of the road. Behind him, the rear of the car sagged ominously.

Near his feet there was a tentative stir.

"Have we stopped?" Vicky quavered.

She was still rolled into a frightened ball underneath the dashboard, and Simon could see by the light of the dome bulb which had proved Uzdanov's undoing that her eyes were not yet open.

"We've stopped temporarily, at any rate," he answered. "But don't move until I tell you to."

Vicky's eyes popped open.

"Don't move?" she objected with a sudden bravado born of the simple realization that she was still alive. "Don't move? Why not?"

"I'll tell you in a minute."

Vicky looked less brave and stared towards the back of the car.

"Is that commie out cold? I think you killed him."

"Anyway, he's resting in peace at the moment," Simon told her, after a cautious twist and a downward glance.

Vicky's expression became a little happier again.

"You almost knocked his head off. It was wonderful."

The Saint was paying much more attention to the precarious position of his car than to his desultory dialogue with Vicky, which was mainly designed to keep her occupied while he decided what to do. If she suddenly realized how close the car might be to losing its balance and dropping over the cliffside, she would be liable to panic and trigger just that undesirable event.

"He almost cut my head off, which wouldn't have been so wonderful," he mentioned abstractedly.

"He's still got my letter!" Vicky remembered aloud.

Before she could unwind herself from the floor the Saint stopped her with a gentle but undeniably firm hand on her shoulder.

"I asked you not to move," he said in a voice that had all the smooth poise of a tightrope-walker's bearing.

"Not move?" Vicky asked indignantly, albeit impressed by his tone. "I want out. From now on I travel by bicycle or I don't travel at all."

"I think you'll be travelling by foot for quite a distance, if we get out of here."

He had chosen the last phrase deliberately.

"*If?*" Vicky echoed uneasily. "Aren't we safe? We're alive and that red rat or whatever he is has got his knife out of our backs. Don't tell me something else can go wrong now?"

Simon nodded and held her eyes magnetized with the intense translucency of his blue ones as he measured his next words.

"What else can be wrong is the fact that the parking place I've ended up in is something less than ideal. Our rear wheels, my dear, are hanging over the void, and it may be only that extra bit of strudel you ate for dinner that's keeping our front end anchored to the road. I recommend that we open our respective doors carefully and jump out simultaneously on the count of three."

Vicky's eyes were very, very wide.

"You're kidding me," she complained weakly.

"If you think so, let me get out first," Simon answered.

"Oh, no! I'll take your word for it."

"Okay, then. Get out when I say 'three'. One . . ."

"Wait!" she said. "What about him?"

"You mean Boris the back-seat driver? We'll let Father Marx worry about him. After all, the car *may* not go over even after we get out."

Vicky's fingers were touching the streak of blood on her cheek.

"I'm not worried about his health," she said. "But he's got that letter he took away from me a few minutes ago. He's got my ten million dollars!"

"We might shift the balance too much if we tried to get it. Worry about saving yourself first, and then worry about your loot." His voice became imperative, still without losing its firm core of calmness. "Now pay attention to what I'm telling you! It's important that we both get out of here at the same time, just in case it takes the two of us weighting down the front of this beetle to keep it from tangling with the thick end of this alp. Open your door while I count, and jump exactly when I say 'three'."

A fresh gust of wind seemed to make the car tremble as he spoke; and Vicky's face, pale in the dim yellow dome light, became rigid with fear.

"Jump," she repeated huskily, her lips barely moving.

"Yes, and be sure you don't jump towards the back of the car or you'll probably go over the edge. The rear end is sticking out into space."

"All right," she responded faintly.

"Good. Get ready, and when I say 'three' get out fast. One . . ."

Simon opened his door slowly, and Vicky timidly did the same.

"Two . . ."

Vicky moved from her kneeling position on the floor to a half-sitting crouch that would let her move quickly out of the car when the last number was called. Her shift of weight, combined with sail-effect of the open doors as they were caught by the wind, made the car sway like a distressed canoe. Her facial hue had become more green than white.

"Oh, we can't!" she whimpered.

Even the Saint felt as if some intestinal quicksand was sucking down the floor of his stomach, but he managed to keep any hint of his sensations out of the timbre of his voice.

"We can," he said resolutely. "Ready? Starting back at one . . . two . . . *three!*"

He gave Vicky a moment's handicap, and then as she threw herself out of her open door he leaped from the driver's seat on to the tumbled stones of the safety wall that the back end of the Volkswagen had smashed through. Just inches from his feet was the deeper blackness of the void which would have welcomed him down if he had slipped. He scrambled away from the lip of the cliff around the front of the car, where Vicky stumbled into his arms. Her whole body trembled against him.

"I almost fell over," she panted. "I didn't know we were so close to the edge."

She was staring up at him with eyes like luminous saucers, and abruptly he was reminded that they were standing in the full brilliance of the Volkswagen's headlights. He turned, helping the girl stay on her feet in spite of her shaky knees, to see what would happen next to the car.

To his surprise, nothing was happening. Even with all the weight of Uzdanov and the engine in its rear, and with the ballast of two bodies removed from its front, the little automobile still clung like a determined insect to the ledge. It is possible that the malevolent spirit of Mischa Ruspine, still smarting from recent intrusion of Comrade Uzdanov's dagger between the shoulder-blades of his mortal clay, was hovering somewhere nearby, and that he had some influence with the wind, for another hefty puff of night air came around the side of the mountain and made the metal under-belly of the car creak shrilly against the rock on which it rested.

But even that was not enough, and the car still stuck on the verge of the precipice.

"What'll we do?" Vicky asked desperately, not loosening her hold on him.

"About Uzdanov?"

"About my money," she corrected him impatiently.

"Well, I'm not one to ignore the call of ten million dollars in distress," he conceded. "Wait here."

"No, you can't—it's too dangerous!" she cried; but she stood back and watched, making no move to stop him.

He walked around the passenger's side of the car so as to get the glare of the headlights out of his eyes, studied the situation, and picked up a large slab of rock which had been knocked loose from the shattered guard wall. He carried it back to the front of the car and wedged the sixty-pound piece of granite on top of the bumper. The counter-weight might help to balance the car on its uncertain fulcrum, or at least it would do something to steady it.

The Saint returned to the driver's side of the car. When he had exited from the driver's seat there had only been about two feet of ground available to him between the open door and the edge of the precipice. Now it looked even less. The door shook in a fresh gust of wind. He touched it delicately, putting no pressure on it, and edged between it and the border of the cliff. Stones displaced by his feet clattered over the side and continued to fall for so long that there was no sound of their landing.

The dome light of the car was still on, and the reflected illumination of the headlights made the interior even brighter. Uzdanov was slumped face down, half on the back seat and half on the floor, his head towards Simon. On the back seat was a piece of unfolded paper, the letter of credit that the Russian had snatched from Vicky.

Simon did not need to get all the way into the car in order to retrieve it, but if the Volkswagen should decide to let go

and fall he would be swept over with it by the open door.
For that reason he gently closed the door again, grateful
that the letter was in no less accessible a place. Bracing himself carefully, not wanting to touch the car at all if he could
help it, he leaned in through the open window, over
Uzdanov's back, until he could catch the letter between
the tips of two fingers.

Then, as he was pulling away, Uzdanov suddenly came
to clumsy life. The portly Russian heaved himself up, his
round face a swamp of blood, and stabbed out for Simon's
eyes with two stiff spread fingers.

Simon jumped back, dodging the jab, and instinctively
grasped the side of the open window as his feet slipped in
the loose rubble on the road shoulder. He used that hold to
regain his balance and haul his body around away from the
chasm and back towards the road. And he would always be
able to claim that he had no time to ponder the Newtonian
corollary that the action which saved him would produce
an equal and opposite reaction on the combined mass of
the car and Comrade Uzdanov . . .

His swing back from the treacherous rim of the shoulder
had a torque effect on the door which overbalanced the
weight of the rock he had placed on the front bumper, and
as he stumbled crabwise to safety the Volkswagen shud-
dered and shrieked metallically against stone, sliding away
like a ship launched into nowhere.

Its headlight beams hove suddenly skyward, and it
slipped away into the dark void in somehow amazing silence. A long time seemed to pass after it disappeared before the brief sounds of crumpling metal and exploding
glass announced its arrival in regions far below.

It was very dark where Simon stood now, and he inched
forward cautiously to peer over the cliffside.

The view was more spectacular than he had expected.
The car had apparently plunged through some high-tension

electric lines as it cracked up at the bottom of the ravine. Its brave headlights still unbelievably on, it was enveloped in blue sparks and orange flashes, like a medium-sized Catherine wheel giving a solo fireworks display at the far end of somebody's garden, for several seconds before the scintillations coalesced into one expanding ball of fire . . .

Simon heard Vicky's awed voice not far behind him.

"You'd have to be a Saint to live through more than one experience like this in a lifetime," she said. "I don't care about the money anymore. Just get me down off this mountain."

"You'll feel a little more materialistic after a ten mile hike and a hot bath." He could see her now in the light of the stars and a rising moon. "Don't waste any remorse on Comrade Uzdanov. He only got something like he'd certainly have dished out to us after he'd gotten all he wanted."

He handed her the piece of paper he had retrieved from the car and then put his arm around her shoulders and gave her an encouraging squeeze.

"Here's your ten million dollars back—but be more careful this time. If you lose this, I'll have to cut down your allowance."

"What'll the police think when they find the car?"

"Let's see . . . It could possibly still be identified as the one I hired, but I'll already have reported it stolen. All we have to do is get back to Geneva without attracting attention. What Inspector Edval thinks then won't really matter. The only evidence shows that Uzdanov, the car thief, had an unfortunate accident, and there's no proof that we were there."

They began to walk slowly down the mountain road.

"Simon," Vicky said wickedly. "Why couldn't we keep *all* the letters for ourselves?"

He took his arm from around her.

"My dear girl! I'm shocked. My ethics may be rather,

shall we say, specialized, but they're the only ones I've got —and I might add among the last genuine handmade ones in the world. Besides which, when I hand them over to Colonel Wade's corresponding number here, the Embassy will have to help us cover any awkward time we can't account for."

She sighed and they went on walking.

A minute later she spoke again.

"Simon," she said worriedly.

"Yes?"

"I don't know what to *do* with ten million dollars."

The Saint threw back his head and laughed, as only one with a fresh ten million dollars of his own can laugh.

"You're the first female I ever heard thinking of that as a problem," he said.

"But I'm going to have to account for how I got it."

"You've got some good practical Middle Western sense behind that pretty face, after all," he said soberly. "You can't suddenly start throwing it around like a drunken oil heiress. It'll take a bit of patient organization to give it a nice legitimate background. But don't worry. I'll be glad to help you work something out, at no extra charge."

He took her arm again, and they walked more quickly down the mountain towards the glow of Geneva in the distance.

LESLIE CHARTERIS

THE SAINT BIDS DIAMONDS

It really was the most remarkable sight. There, caught in the car headlights on a cobbled road in Tenerife, three large villainous men were engaged in beating the living daylights out of one elderly gent and a young woman

Not the sort of incident that Simon Templar and Hoppy Uniatz could just pass by. Yet the results were to be not at all what they might have expected.

No gratitude from the damsel in distress, but deep suspicion. No quiet thanks from the silver haired man, but a great outcry about a missing paper. And no injured innocence as the Saint realises he is in the presence of a man who had taken part in one of the great jewel thefts of all time.

POST A LITTLE HAPPINESS

Post·A·Book

A Royal Mail service in association with the Book Marketing Council & The Booksellers Association.

Post-A-Book is a Post Office trademark.

LESLIE CHARTERIS

THE SAINT'S GETAWAY

The Saint had made a most saintly vow. He had promised both Patricia Holm and his old friend Monty: no more trouble.

Which was why the three of them were on holiday together in Austria, enjoying a relaxed, after-dinner stroll beside the river when they chanced upon the fight.

With iron self-control, Simon Templar held back for all of ninety seconds before launching himself into the fray.

Of course had he known then that before the night was out he would have found a dead man in his hotel bedroom, crossed swords with his old adversary Prince Rudolf and got himself involved in the theft of half the Montenegrin crown jewels, he might have hesitated longer.

Or leaped in sooner.

HODDER AND STOUGHTON PAPERBACKS

LESLIE CHARTERIS

THE SAINT GOES WEST

Simon Templar waited. The blazing Arizona sun beat
down on the bare rock of the hills. Narrowing his
eyes, he could see out in the desert, a billowing line
of dust creeping along the dirt trails and heading his
way.

So far The Saint was legal. In his pocket was his state-
issued hunting licence. But the game he was hunting
was much bigger that anything seen before out West.
Game with international dimensions. Game that was
no game at all but deadly serious.

Slowly, as the car laboured up the slope towards him,
he raised his .357 Magnum and took aim . . .

HODDER AND STOUGHTON PAPERBACKS

MORE SAINT TITLES AVAILABLE FROM HODDER AND STOUGHTON PAPERBACKS

All these books are available at your local bookshop or newsagent, or can be ordered direct from the publisher. Just tick the titles you want and fill in the form below.

Prices and availability subject to change without notice.

Hodder & Stoughton Paperbacks, P.O. Box 11, Falmouth, Cornwall.

Please send cheque or postal order, and allow the following for postage and packing:

U.K. – 55p for one book, plus 22p for the second book, and 14p for each additional book ordered up to a £1.75 maximum.

B.F.P.O. and EIRE – 55p for the first book, plus 22p for the second book, and 14p per copy for the next 7 books, 8p per book thereafter.

OTHER OVERSEAS CUSTOMERS – £1.00 for the first book, plus 25p per copy for each additional book.

Name ....

Address ....

....